Praise for

Rob Walker

Rob Walker has produced a delightful cross-genre melee ... sometimes bucolic, sometimes heartwarming and homespun and sometimes apocalyptic, but always engaging and thought-provoking, taking the reader into different times and places, always with an eye to opening perception.

~ Magdalena Ball, editor of *Compulsive Reader*

Walker's eclectic collection of short stories and poems takes us on a wild ride across a staggering diversity of cultures and genres. With a keen eye for the details of life and language, Walker takes delight in delving into the myriad and unexpected ways that light and dark can coexist in each of us.

~ Rachael Mead, poet, and author of *The Flaw in the Pattern*

He's a bit of a humble treasure, hidden away. His short fiction, memoir and essays have appeared in *Bewildering Stories*, *Zodiac Review*, *Transnational Review*, *Stringybark Books* and *Short and Twisted*. So here he is – medium height, unembittered, but still pretty twisted – which is why I like him.

~ Peter Goldsworthy, award-winning writer of short stories, poetry, novels and opera libretti

Don't tell me Rob Walker is mellowing! In this mixed-genre collection he explores the need for tolerance: for monks who can't quite shake off their worldly desires, to a 3XL cosplay girl who doesn't fit in, even for a retired banker. But don't worry, he still gets in a few barbs along the way; shifting from the deadly serious to the satiric to the empathetic and sometimes even daring to celebrate joy.

~ Mike Ladd, poet, author and broadcaster

Rob Walker is more than a poet. He's an observer, a street philosopher with a microscopic eye for the beauty, the irony and the possibilities in everyday life that escape the less observant. In one of my favourite stanzas from this book Rob tells us that occasionally we come to an intersection in life where no choice is the wrong one. In this case, I urge my fellow square pegs to choose to dive into this fabulous collection. You will be rewarded.

~ Stephen Dando-Collins, author of *Heroes of Hamel*

Rob Walker reveals the breadth of his talents in this quirky collection of fiction, memoir and poetry. This is a book of journeys: on foot, bus, train and spaceship, from ancient past into distant future, from Australia to Japan and back again. Walker is our whimsical guide, moving effortlessly between the grounded normality of childhood memory and the surreal fantasy of an imagined future. An insightful dissection of contemporary morality that bristles with humour and humanity.

~ Alison Flett, poetry editor of *Transnational Literature*

SQUARE PEGS

ROB WALKER

TRUTH SERUM PRESS

ISBN: 978-1-925536-62-1

Truth Serum Press
32 Meredith Street
Sefton Park SA 5083
Australia

Email: truthserumpress@live.com.au
Website: https://truthserumpress.net
Truth Serum Press catalogue: https://truthserumpress.net/catalogue/

Author photograph by Martin Christmas
Cover design by Matt Potter

Also available as an eBook
ISBN: 978-1-925536-63-8

Truth Serum Press is a member of the
Bequem Publishing collective
https://www.bequempublishing.com/

for those who don't quite fit …

Contents

— a miscellaneous hotchpotch of short fiction, poems, memoir and assorted writings about non-conformists, freaks, eccentrics, individualists, ugly ducklings, mavericks, lone wolves and losers

Tolerance

I am Tan zan.

In my forty seventh year I gave my modest home to my wife and set off to lead the wandering life of a monk.

The twenty years that have come and gone since are travellers, like me. My home is now a long road that has no end. Along it are the places I have lain my misshapen head, the minutes and days but stone markers along the side of that narrow path. The people I have encountered, the Wonders of Nature and moments bestowed upon me are more precious than the gold and jade of Emperors.

I had spent a few weeks in the generous company of the monks of Matsue Castle Town. One of the younger Brothers, Ekido, expressed his wish to join me in my pilgrimage to the Holy Shrine of Ise. It had been my wish for many years to complete this journey of faith to serve our Lord Buddha. A younger companion would ease the loneliness and allow me to share joys and privations which might well last more than the Four Seasons.

And so, having prepared a coat of paper, a cotton yukata for summer and a tatami straw cape to keep off some of the rain, we set off on the Twenty Seventh day of The Tenth Moon, in the Thirty Second Year of Genroku.

We left just before dawn, with the autumn sky as soft and misty as the shores of Lake Shinji in rain. We must have looked a comical pair, both in black robes, with shaved heads; his head smooth, like a mushroom, mine bumpy like a Summer melon left till Winter. He, tall and handsome as a bamboo, I, short and gnarled as a neglected old plum tree. My companion, thirty years my junior, was more heavily laden. He wanted to be prepared for anything that Fate might throw at him.

We can never be thus prepared.

We divided the mochi and daikon that our farewelling brothers had given us. Ekido had a rather larger pack on his back and extra clothing.

It seems to me that I have had many advantages dedicating my life to God later in life. I was blessed with children and a good wife. I had made a good deal of money to provide for my wife and grown children. A life of celibacy and poverty is not to be entered without much thought.

Young Ekido was little more than a youth. He was hard-working and devout, but had little tolerance for others who were not. He had taken vows of celibacy at a time when his body yearned for the flesh of another. Perhaps this fuelled his occasional flashes of anger. There were times he would go off into the forest and I suspect, though it is not for me to judge, spill his seed on the ground.

As we headed generally south, the rising sun warmed our left cheeks. Ekido was testy during that first morning. He wanted to put as many ri behind us as possible by nightfall. He became impatient with my old bones. He would surge ahead, angry that I couldn't keep up, then wait, annoyed that I wasn't there yet. He rarely spoke, but his deep sighs and clicking tongue spoke to me loudly. I suppose at his age I too grew frustrated by old men.

In the afternoon we passed through The Forest Of Giant Bamboo That Talks. This forced my friend to slow his pace.

Perhaps he was less experienced at stepping through the roots and choosing the Path of Ease, which is often not a straight line. The weight of extra possessions brought droplets of sweat to his brow, which resembled a paddy-field before planting. His pack was wider than his shoulders and turning sidewards did not help. Twice he misjudged the space so that his belongings were a double-burden, causing him to fall heavily.

I recited old waka and sang folk songs to cheer him. The poetry failed, but my singing voice was so bad that he began to laugh. Then a breeze sprang up. The leaves over our heads washed like the waves of the Inland Sea and the bamboo trunks hit together, clattering the xylophone music of Nature.

Soon we came out of the bamboo to a clearing with a small stream. God had provided. Following the twitterings of small finches, we found berries we could eat with our mochi and bamboo shoots and bountiful water beside which we camped.

I awoke, refreshed. My makeshift bed of bamboo leaves had taken me some time to collect the previous evening, but rewarded me with a good night's sleep. Ekido had been irritable at the end of our first day and too tired to gather leaves.

This morning, he didn't complain aloud, but I noticed he limped all morning and his eyes were those of a fox at night.

I remembered there was a hot-spring onsen along the path to the valley. I thought it may help Ekido's aches, so we sought it out. We found the onsen. Alas, the Earth had moved over the Seasons and the water had been poisoned. Hot, poisonous vapours spewed from vents, smelling worse than the monks' latrine after Onion Festival. Dead bees and moths carpeted the barren volcanic sands around the spring.

I have always felt that it is better to offer Long Life to everything – except Disappointment. Is there anything to be gained by regretting the past? Why kick the thorns that scratch you? What is simply is.

Perhaps God has a purpose in poisoned hot springs.

People say the mosquito is useless and a blight upon the Earth.

But the frog, the bat, and the dragonfly may disagree.

Perhaps Ekido would learn this one day.

This was not the day.

Down-wind from the springs we came upon a copse of magnificent pines with raised roots. It was as if the soil had been washed away to the height of a man and exposed the roots of these old giants. They appeared to be standing on the tips of their toes to gain a better view.

I saw then that poisonous onsen do have a purpose. These pines had been sculpted by the hand of The Master Gardener. On one side of each tree the new tips had been pruned by the toxic mists, like windswept cliff trees moulded by salt winds. The shapes produced were pleasing, like the curves of a beautiful woman.

Soon the path became even narrower, wending into a valley engulfed by dark pines. It was cold in here. Dew dripped from the mosses growing on exposed roots and trunks.

It was clear that we could not get through this vast forest before the sun fell to earth. We needed a dry place for the night. The path continued to narrow. I judged it to be rarely used except perhaps by the occasional hunter or woodcutter. Ekido began to predict that we would die of the cold or starvation this very night.

"Yes, we might," I replied. "Or we may not."

When it appeared that our path might peter out completely like a guttering candle on a dark night, we turned a corner around a large smooth boulder and our tiny path intersected a wider road. Not more than fifty paces ahead stood an old cottage, falling down in places. A curl of blue woodsmoke welcomed us like a beckoning finger.

This was not an Inn, but the poor owner would not turn us away as the evening air chilled and he warmed us with hot miso soup. I noticed the bowl was cracked. I would give him my begging-bowl before I left.

It was indeed a poor and wretched place. After our soup there was thunder without and a heavy downpour. Inside there were fleas, mosquitoes and the roof leaked. Ekido was complaining about our luck so I gave him my corner, which seemed a little drier.

I was so exhausted from our day's walk that I fell asleep immediately.

Some hours later I awoke – although at first it seemed it was a dream. The rain had eased and a full moon shone on my face from the slatted window-opening. The frogs were singing. There were voices drifting through the rice-paper shoji screen to the only other room. They were the voices of young women. The voice of an older man – perhaps the kind owner – mingled with theirs. These guests must have arrived after we had fallen asleep.

I gathered they were ladies of pleasure. They had the practised, girlish giggles of geisha- or maiko-san. I fell asleep, their chatter forming part of my pleasant dreams.

In the morning Ekido's spirits were low. Water had leaked in during the night, leaving a puddle on the earthen floor which seemed to be restricted to Ekido's corner of the room.

One of the young women approached us.

"We are lost. We know not the way. We wish to pray at the Holy Shrine of Ise!"

I smiled and told them we shared their destination.

Ekido blushed and scowled.

"Please extend to us your priestly Mercy and Compassion so that we too may be blessed by The Buddha! All we ask is to follow you at a discreet distance."

It is not for me to judge.

I nodded.

Ekido almost choked on his radish.

We left after a simple meal of boiled rice. I gave our kind host a bowl and my summer kimono.

The young ladies kept their promise, following about fifty paces behind, although Ekido looked behind often, to be sure. They would not have made good hunters. Even in the denser parts of the momiji forest their voices could be heard carolling like the dawn chorus. When we stopped for water they almost stumbled over us and covered their nervous giggles with their white-gloved hands, overtaking us in an arc to avoid conversation and embarrassment.

At the next bend in the road it was we who surprised them. The girls had reached the intersection of two well-trodden paths. The tracks had turned to rivulets during the night and their confluence was now a small lake.

The first girl had braved the depths. She waited forlornly on the other side, taking off her muddied geta and white toed-stockings, now soaked and filthy. The second girl, in a fine silk kimono the colour of wisteria, looked across through tears that pooled in her eyes. These tears seemed destined to join the huge puddle below.

"Wait!" I yelled. I ran and scooped her up, wading across in my sandals which could become no muddier in any event. Her waist reminded me of my own daughter's, so many years ago. She had almost no weight at all.

Perhaps her weight had been transferred to Ekido. He seemed to carry a great burden for the rest of the day.

By fall of night we had reached The Temple of the Burning Bower. It was then that Ekido gave me his lesson in morality.

"We monks don't go near females. Especially not young and lovely ones. It is dangerous. Why did you do that?"

"I left the girl there," I said. "Are you still carrying her?"

Ekido flushed hotly. I could have added that a young celibate and pious monk would not even have noticed that she was young and lovely.

But there was nothing to be gained.

He will be cured of his intolerance.

All he need do is wait thirty years.

Bo Peep

Bo Peep lit the end of the hand-made cigarette in her left hand. Her vermilion cupid-bow lips sucked heavily on the lumpy paper tube. Loose strands of tobacco ignited and the red glow raced crackling towards her tongue. She couldn't find the tailor-mades since government taxes had driven the tobacco companies to the wall. No more *Hope* or *Peace*. Now it was all imported black market weed she rolled herself. Rice paper worked well. She drew in a lungful and pushed the smoke out of her mouth, inhaling it over her upper lip into her nostrils, time-lapse water over smooth stones. Within seconds the nicotine was burning into her alveoli and being absorbed into her bloodstream.

Smoking, though socially unacceptable, was not yet totally banned. Like many of the older cosplay girls she was addicted but there was a tolerance for eccentric behaviour here in Yoyogi Park that didn't exist in other parts of Japan. She was 25 now, but still quite slim. The cigarettes helped.

Her right hand held the white satin-wrapped shepherd's crook, the symbol of her Character. Her hair was dyed blonde and permed so that curls cascaded from under her pink polka-dot bonnet, her small breasts flattened even more by the white silk bodice.

It was then that she saw the Fat Girl.

Deviation was accepted here on the weekends. It was a relief-valve for the high-pressure conformity of the machine called Tokyo. Without it the entire apparatus might explode into its component parts.

But this was going too far.

The girl was no more than seventeen. She wore a black micro-mini skirt. Tiny in length but massive in width, the two adipose buttocks wobbling as she ambled through the park. Her corpulent dimpled thighs wobbled in waves with each step, ripples reflected from a swimming pool's edge. But above was worse. Her bikini top did little more than cover her protruding nipples, the pendulous breasts drooping down like soggy soap hanging in a net bag. Her midriff exposed, the expansive belly overflowing the straining belt, overhanging her skirt like some repulsive fleshy verandah.

Obesity had almost been wiped out in the 2020s. Occasionally unfortunate overweight individuals with glandular dysfunction could be seen on the fringes — sometimes the homeless from the nearby camps who were unable to afford liposuction. They skulked in shadows, ashamed but well-covered.

But here she was — young and brazen — flaunting her fat for all to see, head erect, clear eyes firmly ahead, well-padded jaw held high. And for the briefest of seconds Bo Peep felt herself attracted to her, fascinated by the sumptuous sensual flesh as The Girl sashayed through Yoyogi Park, a supersized belly dancer.

Perhaps it was to assuage her own guilt at seeing beauty in this abomination. For whatever reason, it was Bo Peep who picked up the pebble from the edge of the gravel footpath at the hem of her blue ruffled bloomers and aimed it at the confident face. It bounced off harmlessly, but the shocked hurt in Fat Girl's eyes burned into Bo Peep's brain. For the rest of her life she would remember that it was she who had cast the first stone.

Bo Peep's pebble was the first. Other girls joined in. The stones became fist-sized and more frequent as the beautiful cosplay girls showed their distaste at the gross interloper who had polluted their public catwalk.

The Girl fell to her knees, assumed the foetal position like some monster embryo pummelled unconscious by this hard rain.

No one knows at what particular point she exhaled her final breath.

There was no one person responsible for her death at the premature age of seventeen. After a brief investigation, no charges were laid.

The mob soon forgot the incident. The young girls returned to what they did best – looking young, fresh and innocent.

Lines written on the train between Himeji and Shirahama

feeling nostalgic listening to old joan baez on the ipod. the world plays out as a foreign movie with the wrong soundtrack. there is no hero or heroine and no real plot. just a cast of walk-on extras. they could be in any city in the world except that mine is the only face that isn't japanese. opposite is Man Who's Still Sleeping Off Last Night's Excesses. enter Man 2 Who's Heading For The Job He Hates But One Day They'll Recognize His Talents And His Boss Will Get The Humiliation He So Richly Deserves. right next to Young Girl Who Has Her First Job And Can Finally Afford The Make-up And Trendy Clothes She's Always Wanted.

and they'll all make their entrances and exits seamlessly without need of reshoots. Denim-Jacket Uni Student stands shoulder-to-shoulder with the Immaculately-Dressed Businessman he abhors and swears he will never become and doesn't realize yet that in twenty years he will.

and they all try to ignore each other and forget the fact that they're all in the same movie. but they swing to the right hanging from their straps as the train lurches and brace for the complete halt at Mega in complete unison, no more independent than a hive of bees.

and the giggling schoolgirls in the skirts they've hitched up are old enough to be loud and confident in a group and very aware of their budding sexuality but not yet wary or disillusioned like the Men in Suits who fantasize about highschool girls in short dresses on trains.

and some people close their eyes because they couldn't go to sleep last night and some close their eyes to avoid the eyes of others and some close their eyes to hide the pain.

and their scarves muffle out the cold and put a stop to mingling white clouds of conversation and the smoke and steam from the refinery billows up from behind towering buildings as some dodgy remake of 9/11.

and Old Man looks with disdain at Feminized Teenage Boy With Bouffant Hair and Bouffant Collar and wonders how, sixty years after Kamikaze pilots, the nation could come to this and produce these slim-hipped, fine-boned fops in hairclips and Boy in Hair Clip just feels sorry for Old Man who's lost all spontaneity and sense of fun.

and the train pulls into Shirahama and i must exit, forever wondering what happens to all of these characters so inter-related   so separate

so desolate.

Mirror

It was just an ordinary mirror that Norman bought from Ikea. After he'd picked it out from the fully furnished display bathroom and written down the catalogue number with the little pencil they'd provided he shuffled to the warehouse and found it wrapped amongst hundreds of identical flatpack clones.

Yesterday the old one had crashed to the floor. Splintered into hundreds of irregular shards. He'd seen the O of his mouth reflected up off the bathroom floor in multiple fractures. *Seven years bad luck they say.* Not that Norman believed that superstitious guff. His mother would have wrapped it in brown paper before disposal. *Nonsense.* He'd put the pieces in an old shoe box out of consideration for the rubbish-handlers, tape it up and add it to the weekly collection. *All those little pieces of my mouth gone to landfill...*

The following day his shave seemed different. The mirror was hanging on the same hook, same morning light coming in from the window at the side. But the reflection was clearer somehow. Better quality perhaps.

He found himself studying his forty year old face with more interest. *Look at those long whiskers under my chin. Must've been missing them for a while.*

He got up close. Became aware of an intimacy as if his own reflection were someone else. You're still quite good looking he said aloud, his lips almost touching their own reflection. Fascinated by his own lips as if seeing them for the first time.

Ba ba ba...

Baa baa black sheep...

He savoured the childhood words, spellbound by the lips and tongue so close to his own.

It was then that his universe tilted. A fundamental paradigm shift which only he could experience.

An outside observer would have noticed nothing in that bathroom on that morning. But Norman's world changed. His reflection said *Not bad for forty...*

Norman's lips moved in unison with the reflection. But Norman **knew**. Knew with the conviction of everyday reality that his image had initiated the words, not him.

He stared at himself in the mirror for an inordinate measure of time, frozen.

Finally he took a breath. *What?* The fog from the *wh-* condensed on the glass and faded just as rapidly. The reflected lips echoed the word. *You heard* they said as Norman's lips slavishly emulated. *I am your reflection* they whispered. It was a mundane conversation. A casual onlooker might have thought Norm's behaviour a little unusual but otherwise the scene followed all the laws and conventions of Light and Physics. Only in Norman's mind could a real conversation between two distinct entities be distinguished.

Am I going mad? Norman wondered aloud. *Don't be ridiculous* said his image. *You're as sane as ever and you know it.* And Norm realised that he was.

It was the first of many morning chats. After the initial shock it wasn't disconcerting for Norman at all. In fact the Other Norman was quite nourishing for his self-esteem. Norm had previously had doubts about his appearance and abilities. Norm Two reassured him and boosted his confidence.

'I've been thinking of going for a promotion' Norm murmured one Tuesday morning before work. *And why not?* said his alter-ego. *You're better than those other drones at the office. Time you got some recognition for all those unrewarded years.* Norm knew in his heart he was right.

He'd often had ideas to improve procedures in the workplace. He'd mentioned one to Gerald over the photocopier one afternoon. Every time they ran out of paper a new box was purchased. Norm checked the accounts and noticed that the brand, the quality and the price fluctuated wildly. Why couldn't they just calculate what was needed on an annual basis, agree on a standard quality and buy in bulk from the lowest tender? Gerald shrugged.

Two weeks later Gerald was congratulated in a General Staff Memo for his "brilliantly innovative cutting-edge idea". A new Understanding on Improving Certain Efficiency Outcomes was to be employed. It included annual bulk-purchasing of paper supplies. Norm was upset. *He's been using you for years* said his reflection. A further two weeks later Gerald was given a promotion to head the newly-formed Efficiencies Implementation Unit. Norm was livid. *Don't get mad* said Norm Two evenly. *Get even.*

It might well have ended right there with Norm resentful but resigned. Perhaps it was Fate. Are events simply random? Does synchronicity really happen?

Norm was at work late and alone. The flexi-hours policy meant that he would often work for one or two hours more on some evenings. It enabled him to complete difficult reports without being interrupted by inane chatter or having to wait for printers to be free. He was particularly bitter this evening as he had just completed an efficiency report instigated by Gerald which used many of the ideas that Norm himself had voiced over the years. He found the last few typos, sent it from his computer to the copier then walked downstairs to the printing room to watch the twenty copies of the stapled report feed out of the printer.

"A Report on Certain Suggested Improved and Streamlined Efficiency Outcomes. Gerald Bolt, Convenor."

As each bound copy clunked onto the sorting tray the words **Gerald Bolt** screamed at Norm. *The ruthless conniving bastard.* After copy three, the machine stopped. Norman looked at the keypad. The warning light was indicating a jam. He opened the top. There was no jam in the rollers or the main feed. The blue lights indicated that there was A4 paper in all of the feed trays, but number three was flashing. He opened the tray. Plenty of paper. He took it out, riffled the stack, put it back. The printing continued.

After one more completed document the copier jammed again. This is bloody ridiculous, he muttered. Sixteen copies to go. If this kept happening he'd miss his train. Gerald had special privileges with his new role. He was entitled to work "offsite." He's probably being paid to sit at home right now and drink a bottle of good red...

He saw his reflection in the photocopier glass. *It's OK. You can do this.*

Calmly he opened the tray, removed the paper and looked inside. There was a tiny stainless steel clip or guide which hadn't returned and was stopping the next sheet from loading. It looked like it just needed a flick with something pointy and the spring would return it to its proper position. The only thing he could see in the room was a paperclip, which he straightened. He touched the wire to the stainless steel.

An unseen hand punched him. He was thrown backwards with two loud involuntary guttural grunts forced from his lungs, the first from the king hit of electricity, the second when he was slammed into the side of the filing cabinet.

'Christ,' said Norm. 'I've been electrocuted.' Immediately his reflection replied *but you survived...* As he sat on the floor, his back to the cabinet and willing himself to slow his hyperventilation Norman realised that now he didn't need to see his reflection to hear him.

He went into the washroom and splashed his face. 'I could have died! I should report this!' he screamed at the mirror. The mirror replied quietly *It might be better if we didn't...*

The next day Norman had to wait almost all day to choose a time when Gerald was in the photocopy room by himself.

'Ahh! Good afternoon Gerald!' he effused with self-satisfying calmness and affability.

'It's probably time we got this machine serviced. I pinpointed a fault last night. Let me show you.'

Norman showed him the trick with the bent paperclip, keeping the wire well away from the faulty part. Then he handed Gerald the straightened paperclip and hurried back upstairs to be with the others.

It was less than three minutes later – just as Norman was putting his coffee cup to his lips – that the lights flickered and died. A few more minutes of pandemonium before a voice from downstairs screamed and it became known that Gerald was dead.

Six months passed and the office was buzzing along as it always had. No-one is indispensable. The parts may expire but the whole continues.

The terrible accidental death of Gerald Bolt had been mourned and grieved over. At the funeral Norm had even given a very nice eulogy about how everyone had benefited from Gerald's initiative and diligence.

Norman was promoted to Gerald's job where he also assumed the role of Convenor of the Occupational Health, Welfare and Safety Task Force. An investigation into that tragic accident concluded that by oversight the photocopier had been plugged into a powerpoint which was part of an old circuit that wasn't connected to the earth leakage circuit breakers installed in the previous fiscal year. Norman would leave no stone unturned in his determination to make the Site a Safe Workplace.

There was no holding Norman back.

Retired banker in a nursing home

you're late he barks.
What branch are you from?
I try to humour him,

this man, unknown to me.
but humour's been withdrawn
such insolence! i'll put you on report!

another day   concluded
doors   closed
books   balanced

but his mind is on probation
a life ledgered in ink of red
or black

his accrued capital
white-anted
grey matter

All these years accounting
for every detail

Now he's overdrawn,
unable to achieve
a final balance.

The River

You can't trust The River. Those romantic scribbles of light on the surface, a silver necklace dancing on black velvet, disguise the fact it's an open sewer. The night-time illusion of depth – stars and moon sucked down into anaerobic mud – cause people to stand on bridges and reflect. They see themselves and their city bouncing back and muse on their lives and insignificance in the greater scheme.

No. The River's a bastard. I should know. I'm The River.

Justin felt himself drawn there. Again. He had some thinking to do. And his legs had just carried him down the gradual descent of the city streets to the wharf. The wharf was a rough port when he was a kid. In those days everything was handled by strong arms, the wharfies, tough union men who took no bullshit. Now it was all containerisation, cranes on rails and robots. The old warehouses were now apartments for the wealthy. But still he found himself pulled towards the water, the reflections, the smells of freshness and putrefaction, the cool breezes and dead fish.

It wasn't Sara's fault. She'd been the best thing that had ever happened to him. Full of life and fun. Her eyes sparkled like this river when she laughed.

So what was his problem?

It was the old self-doubt. The feeling that he didn't deserve Sara. The dread that his secure job with the company would evaporate when They discovered all of his faults. He'd been fooling everyone all his life, hadn't he?

Justin always ended up here when he felt like this. Was it returning to his childhood and happier times? The River expected nothing of him, made no demands. He saw it as a lowest common denominator. The great leveller. It soothed his anxiety. Just staring into its depths helped him to order his thoughts and calm his fears.

A swell came from nowhere. An uplifting, a welling, as if some creature was about to surface. Justin shuddered. The balmy evening suddenly chilled as the cold wind reached through his clothes. As he fastened his top button and turned up his collar, he caught a flash from a street light reflected off The River from the bridge.

The surface had changed.

It was reticulated, like a snake's back or a crocodile. Then he heard the cry of a newborn baby. Impossible. He put his fingers over the edge of the wharf and jumped off. A casual observer – had there been one – might have thought he was throwing himself off the pier. But this had been Justin's manoeuvre since childhood. Five feet underneath the wharf was a solid cross-beam where they used to tie up the tugboats. As a kid he'd walk along the edge of the wharf and – when he was sure no-one was around or watching – he'd swing out of view in a second. Then he was free to scavenge flotsam and jetsam, illegally fish or generally hang out underneath to be by himself. Sometimes at night he'd eavesdrop on the lovers' conversations when they thought they were alone.

Funny how muscle-memory never fades, thought Justin. He hadn't done that for ten years. Repeating the swinging movement he climbed down to the next cross-member, just above the tide.

It wasn't a giant snake or a crocodile — just an old hessian bag breaking the surface. Then the cry. Was it human? Both curiosity and compassion compelled him to stretch out and just manage to get two fingers to a corner of the bag.

The crying had stopped.

But for the distant city rumble and the lapping against the piers, silence.

A tentative untying of baling twine as he held his breath. He wasn't about to put his face near the mouth of the waterlogged bag — or thrust his hand in. He lifted the sack from the water, a dead weight. Still no sound. It was taking forever for the water to drain out and lighten the load. Back under the wharf it was pitch-black. His pulse pounding in his ears, he swung the bag up as gently as he could to the higher cross-beam, but still it landed with a heavy squelch. Then he climbed, repeated the swing up to the wharf and followed the bag.

At least there was some light here.

Justin still wasn't about to put his hand in the bag. He gingerly held the two corners opposite the open end of the sack and tipped the wet contents onto splintered planks.

They were cats. Bloody dead cats. Kittens with matted fur, all their legs and tails tangled in a sad waterlogged mess. Some sick bastard must have tied them in a sack and thrown them off the wharf.

He didn't want to throw them back. The bridge lights twinkled off the matted hair. The remaining water ran off the tiny dead bodies and puddled around them, finding the gaps between the planks and drip, dripping back to The River.

Was that a movement? Justin froze. The mass of dead cats was slowly moving as one. He held his breath, then exhaled quietly, watching and listening. With his heart pounding somewhere in his throat, he touched a tentative toe to this grisly pile. The mound rose, then parted. A head appeared. Then a faint meow. Justin was so relieved he laughed out loud, reaching in and picking up the frightened kitten. It was wet and shivering, but it wasn't drowned. Justin must have spotted the hessian bag soon after it had been dumped. He tucked the tiny creature inside his jacket. By the time he was home it was purring.

One got away. Five out of six isn't bad...

A shiver rippled over the surface of The River.

It was growing stronger.

Justin tried to sneak into the apartment, but Sara was already awake.

'Justin! Where've you been?'

It was a desperate question which sounded angry. The kind of anger which stems from love.

'Sorry, love. You were asleep. I just ducked out for a walk. Thought I'd be back quicker. Nothing usually wakes you.'

'Well it did,' she pouted. 'I've been beside myself!'

'Sorry', he mumbled, reaching into his jacket.

Sara looked puzzled, but less than a minute into his story, she'd melted. The combination of the cute kitten, now dry and fluffy, and her sheepish partner who'd rescued it, reminded her of how much she loved this guy.

After feeding the kitten milk and watching it purr itself to sleep on an old towel in a cardboard carton, Sara and Justin made love slow and long. The most contented either of them had been in months. They fell asleep curled in each others' arms, almost purring like the kitten in the next room.

As he always did after sex, Justin slept like a baby for the rest of the night. Sara awoke after an hour. Or perhaps she was sleep-walking. Justin's story of the matted mass had disturbed her.

What if they weren't all dead?

Without switching on the light, she walked trance-like out of the apartment, leaving the front door wide open. She padded barefoot towards The River, the warm evening breeze pushing her thin cotton nightie against her small breasts and belly. She drifted the one block to the wharf and the warm wind caressed her body as perspiration ran down the inside of her thighs.

The River beckoned her with its cool waters. As inexorable as a magnet drawing iron filings.

Let me enfold you. Give your body to me and I will carry your burden. Sooth your brow. Wash away your cares.

Sara paused a while, seeing the stars and moon swirling in The River below her. Then she stepped off the edge. The River opened and she slid in. Then it closed in around her. It rose in a swell, like a huge animal drawing breath.

Lost one kitten. Gained five kittens. Lost one human, gained a human. It all comes out in the wash…

The River calmed. It was full of energy. Still, yet deep. It reflected the moon and stars. Squiggles shivered over its black surface.

crying at the
poetry reading

there is a poet crying. she read her poem earlier.
now it is not her turn to read. it's her time to cry.

perhaps the cheap cardboard wine loosened a sad memory,
sent it spilling onto the floor, a moan leaking from her eyes.

the other poets ignore her, embarrassed. dictionaries with hair.
bower birds of words. after all, she's had her turn.

besides, they prefer their emotions to be distilled to an essence,
boiled away to leave a black residue on white paper.

The Question

"Isn't it interesting that we haven't really changed the ageing process despite all our tinkering? Now that I'm 40, I've noticed that my body shape has begun to subtly change. Despite all of our modern dietary limitations, exercise regimes, nanobot and reconstructive surgery, I'm still developing the ancient cliché *middle-age spread.* Or *growing gut* as my insubordinate adolescent offspring refer to it."

Milton re-read his first paragraph. It wasn't a bad start. The kind of thing his "readers" (listeners really) had come to expect. Self-deprecating, a dig at the teenage children, not too serious. Perhaps he'd change "insubordinate adolescent offspring" — a little pompous and old-fashioned, and many listeners wouldn't know "insubordinate". That was the essence of his current malaise. Perhaps he could rail at the falling education standards once again. And yet he was part of the problem. Here he was, sitting in front of an antique wordprocessor, punching @ antiquated keys to produce "text" which would be recreated as speech by a cyberactor. Speech and vision accessed by millions of Viewer / Listeners over the next few days. Most of these VLs were highly intelligent, but few would be capable of reading the ancient text that Milton used to compose his musings.

It was happening again. His morose mood had re-erected the barrier formerly called *writer's block.* He reread the opening again. No use. Perhaps a short break...

*   *   *

The apartment was dark and silent except for a soft squawk from Mimi the family dodo. Milton usually worked @ nite.

He wandered down to the *kitchen*, the very word one of extreme embarrassment to his children.

"You're a wealthy, successful Muser, Milton!" they'd despair. (Never *Dad* — NO one did that anymore.) "Why would you want to prepare your own food?" It was true. He could access any online snack and expect delivery within minutes. By touching "time", "place" and "style" onscreen, he could order anything from 1950 New Orleans Cajun crawdads to 2130 Szechwan Retro-Soyburger — that was part of the cause of his expanding waistline — but sometimes he just enjoyed the novelty of simple food preparation.

The fridge revealed a small piece of Apatosaurus fillet, which he reheated. He could hear his children, thankfully asleep in real time, bemoaning "Why do you save stuff, Milton? Leftovers are unhygienic and SO twentieth century. And NOBODY eats dead animal anymore." But Milton still did. He remembered his own father telling him that meat-eating was once common place, and the excitement of tasting rehabilitated endangered species, and later, the farmed clones of the Formerly Extinct.

FEs were quite the rage for a while, with dinner party menus boasting "Thylacine Ribs in Acacia Seed Sauce" and "Raptor Drumsticks Pan-fried in South Australian Olive Oil". But a number of unfortunate pet Thylacine attacks, not to mention the Tyrannosaur Plains incident, had led to a complete State ban on the cloning or farming of all present and past carnivores. "Another positive example of State Intervention," Milton, who was something of a conservative, had written at the time.

The apatosaur was quite acceptable in the usual gamy, proto-reptilian way. Milton autorecycled the container and utensil.

There are so many things wrong, Milton pondered. If only the State would intervene more often. The Golden Years, he mused. Perhaps every generation's own adolescence... He should make a note of that for a future piece. The breakdown of many of the corporatised essential services in the mid-first century had led to massive nationalisation and ultimately State Intervention by century's end. Great times... The State really caring for its people, Localization undoing many of the excesses of Millennial Globalization... Yet now, the 'Laissez-Fairies' were fighting back. Didn't people learn anything from History?

Trouble was, they didn't. Nobody taught history. Or read it. Nobody read. If it wasn't available as a 5sec vidbyte, no-one was interested...

The morbid depression was coming back again. He must fight it. His days as a Philosopher were over. Non-vocational tertiary teaching was as dead as the tyrannosaur. He was a Muser, now. Highly paid to amuse, entertain, divert. He'd make an appointment with the therapist again tomorrow. Milton washed down a fluoxetine with a 2099 McLaren Vale Petit Verdot.

It was more than the gut. That could be fixed with a few Surgery-implanted lipo-scavenger nanobots. He wouldn't even need to take the day off. Follicle regeneration would take care of the thinning patch @ his crown. And with hormone replace-ment and a few more artificial terabytes to augment his memory, there was no conceivable reason why he should ever show any of the outward signs of ageing. He was only 0.4 of the way through his life. His income and education had enabled a special privilege — a State-sanctioned child of each gender. He had been taught from earliest memory that he could stay fit and healthy right up to the day of his 100th birthday when he'd be given 10cc of the Final Solution.

You have everything, Milton, he told himself, staring out-of-focus @ the ancient fridge door. A perfect partner and off-spring... well paid job... yet there's an emptiness like hunger. He patted his abdomen. It's just the Physical reminders of my own mortality...

He couldn't imagine another 60 empty years of writing jaded humour. He pushed the hidden button under the desk and the tray opened. He drew up 10cc of The Solution into the needle. Looking for the vein in the wrist... a river flowing through a bleak landscape.

Who was that Second Millennium writer...?

Then, impulsively, he reached for his cyberpad and hit search. *Hamlet.*

Ah yes... *Shakespeare...*

> *"to be*
> *or not to be.*
> *That is the question..."*

He lay aside the hypodermic on the desk.
Perhaps he'd read the old play just one more time.

onsen song

we exhaust his few words of english and my japanese in the first minute
his thin eighty year old naked body next to my potbellied western
    version in the public bath at taisho pond. he tries to ask me questions
in *nihon-go* and i eventually shrug shoulders protruding from the
      steaming waters. *"Gomenasai. Nihon-go… muzakashii!"*
      (sorry. japanese – too hard!)
         he replies. "no. english muzakashii!" we laugh and
      lapse into a comfortable silence then he drags
    his old body from the supporting arms of water
    and squats on the stool, scrubbing himself all
      over yet again. and begins to hum what i
      guess is a japanese folk song. before long he is
  singing full-throated and his thin speaking voice has
    transformed into a baritone reverberating around
    the stone walls of the onsen as it may have hundreds
    of years ago. i try to memorise the notes to
      reproduce it later but the song now is just
        a memory drifting upwards,
      impossible to hold,
   like steam from
bathwater.

Running out of time

Dying hadn't been half as bad as Zachary expected.

One minute he was on his bicycle running late for the job interview, the next he'd had it, finished, kaput.

Not that he knew it at the time. It was all a little more, well, complicated than that.

The resumé had been perfect, hence making the short-list and the second interview. Then the car hadn't started. He knew the battery was on the way out. The plan had been to buy a new one as soon as he got the new job. No sweat. He still had an hour to get there on his bicycle although he wouldn't have time to change. He'd have to wear the suit, shirt and tie and take it easy so he didn't sweat too much.

He just missed the lights going up Port Road. Bugger. This bloody South Road intersection traffic light cycle took five minutes he didn't have. On the South Road traffic's amber light he slipped the derailleur and stood on the pedals to sneak through... no cops about... A van on his right was braking. It was clear. Only it wasn't clear. A B-Double truck with twenty tons of gravel overtook the van on the outside lane, riding the amber-turned-to-red. Zachary didn't stand a chance.

The ambulance station was just around the corner. That didn't help Zachary.

Zoom in on the grille of the truck. Zachary's life is an infinitely fast slideshow of stills. On impact the camera angle changes to overhead. Zachary's eyes are closed, but he sees himself from directly above.

The man who has come to collect him is wearing a suit, conservative, grey, not a bit like Zachary's, bought from Roger David at the January Sales, now torn and blood-spattered. The man introduces himself as *Jason, your Case Manager.*

'Our first task is to get you out of those.' He says this with kindness, but a hint of distaste.

'If I could just borrow your suit, I might still make the interview,' says Zachary, walking with Jason and checking his watch that stopped five minutes ago.

'Don't worry about the interview. It's been rescheduled. We have a bit of Housekeeping to do. Then we'll deal with the Paperwork.'

They turn right into a gym change room where Jason directs him to shower cubicles. He leaves him with towels and a white tracksuit and shoes.

Zac emerges relieved that he has no physical injuries but still worried about the interview. He needs this job. He needs a new battery. Now he has to buy a new bike. And a new suit, shirt and tie. He can't be late.

After the shower, Jason has gone.

'Hi. I'm Jeremy, your new Case Manager. Before we start I need to tell you that our core business is Customer Satisfaction. I'd appreciate it if later you could complete this Customer Feedback Card regarding my performance.'

'Um, sure. Where do I go for the interview?'

'Counter A. It's not far.'

Counter A isn't too onerous. Zachary has to complete a D43 form which asks questions like previous addresses, religious beliefs (Zac just puts a dash here), DOB and DOD.

They proceed to Meeting Room 102 where they are expected. Zachary sits in the last vacant space in the circle of stackable chairs. After a rather silly game called an Icebreaker, the 'RDs' are asked to introduce themselves.

'What should I say?' asks Zachary.

'You could begin by telling us about your day,' prompts Jeremy helpfully, 'Or perhaps your Personal Goals.'

'That's not easy' says Zachary. 'My goals today keep changing. First I just wanted to make a good impression at the interview. Then my aim was just to get there looking presentable. When I realized I was running late, I stopped worrying about sweating. I just wanted to get there on time. When I saw the grille of the truck I hoped it wouldn't dirty my shirt. Then my objective was not to damage the bike. By the time the truck hit me, I just wanted to live...'

'Well that's not gunna happen is it?' interrupts Kev, a man in dirty overalls, rather indelicately. The others in the circle frown their disapproval.

'Sorry?' says Zac. Kev persists.

'The interview. Ain't gunna happen. Plus you ain't livin'.'

Zac is flustered. The others are suddenly interested in their shoelaces, fingernails and microscopic pieces of lint on their clothes. Kev pushes on.

'Haven't they told you about RDs? We're Recently Deceased. You might wanna re-assess your goals, like *wanting to live* for one.' Kev laughs, but no one joins him.

For Zac, it is as if someone has removed the floor. He is just there. A point floating in space. The other RDs fade into the general whiteness.

'So that's it?' says Zachary. 'Twenty four years and then… and then… it just stops?'

Kev places a meaty hand on Zachary's shoulder.

'That's about the size of it, matey. But don't worry about it now. You don't *need* a job here. All your needs are provided for… And as for wond'rin' what it's all about — what you achieved and that — well, that's why we have these sessions. You've got the whole of bloody Eternity to analyze what you did in those twenty-four years.'

'You could even get a Management Position like Jeremy here. You know — lead Counsellin' Sessions. A new intake's comin' up in a few weeks.'

Zachary relaxes a little. Maybe this isn't so bad after all. He would be starting at the bottom of course, but he could always work his way up. A young guy like him — why, the world was his oyster!

I wonder what I should wear to the interview…

to the homeless Japanese man I watch from the bus every day

You are not stupid,
know where and when the restaurants put out uneaten food,
shopping bags a coloured filing system.

You sit on the morning-sunned bench, feign
waiting for the bus
which will never come.

Take a tiny pair of scissors from the pale green bag,
cut an article of interest from the *Kobe Shimbun*,
fold the rest and put it in the pink bag.

Tonight the newspaper will warm your left leg.
Later today you'll prepare for the right one,
sun bathing you like a lizard in its golden glow.

Your joints loosen. You begin to hum to yourself.
You know the time to start loitering by the supermarket
at closing time to unpack your life.

Too early and you'll be moved on,
too late and some other contender will usurp your space,
in the dark but out of the draught.

Today will be a good day.

The torture of Yahia

I am in a... how you say? chair for haircut. My hands are tied to arms. He uses his right hand to make a band of steel around his left wrist. *Top of legs. Nothing... How you say 'no clothe'?* Naked? *Yes. Head is down.* Yahia puts chin to chest. *Then hot water to your head. Very hot.* Boiling? He nods his bald head. *You see hair falling onto body.* His hands brush lightly down his trunk. *You must keep head down. If you put back, the hot water hit your... is it 'genital'? Very much pain. Put your head back more, it hit the back.* Yahia cups his hand to indicate a headrest *and electric all through your body.*

His body shakes either by way of demonstration or muscle-memory. Juan nods his head. He too knows the effect of electricity through the human body...

Yahia has tears in his eyes. So do I. He pauses, makes a nervous kissing sound with his lips, all the while unconsciously counting omnipresent prayer-beads with his thumb as we would have flicked marbles as kids. I ask him if he ever has nightmares, you know, bad dreams. *No more. There was time I dream about...* He says an Arabic word I don't understand, then reaches up for the dangling cord of the green café umbrella in whose shade we are standing. He loops it over his head and we are in no doubt. Before his escape he had had recurrent dreams about the noose. He knew that his name, Yahia Al-Samawy was on one of Saddam Hussein's execution orders. It was just a matter of time...

We stand in the shade of a London plane tree and a very old palm. *We have this in Iraq, but this one has no fruit...*

47

It is the final day of Adelaide Writers' Week. A perfect autumn day. Some of the glossy green leaves on what might be Manchurian pears have begun their slow turn to the colour of shiraz. Or blood. We are standing between the East tent and the West tent, two giant but temporary marquees set up in a parkland. The dappled March sunshine filters through these deciduous refugees from another continent onto an audience drinking glasses of wine and beer and short blacks in paper cups. It could be a painting by Renoir or Monet...

Perhaps it is not so much impressionism as surrealism, this talk of horror in these leafy surroundings. I mention the irony to Yahia. *People ask me where paradise begins. It is here — in Adelaide.* And where is Hell? *Perhaps it comes from the Pentagon...*

Yahia laughs, showing the false teeth which replace the ones they knocked out.

Juan Garrido-Salgado was born in Chile. A committed socialist, he became Pinochet's political prisoner after "The Other September 11", when democratically-elected president Allende was overthrown in a CIA-assisted military coup and assassinated in 1973. After imprisonment and torture Juan sought exile in Adelaide in 1990. A writer of beautiful poetry in Spanish, he had to begin all over again with this new language, English. The story he was hearing from Yahia had uncomfortable parallels in his own life.

At the beginning of the week it had been hot. Too hot to stand in the sun. Now the late afternoon is cool and the leaves are turning. The world is changing.

Sometimes I have felt my own life has been unexciting, mundane. Same city, same job. A primary school teacher my whole life, it seems. Yet talking to these two freedom-fighters makes me wonder if it's simply fairness and predictability to which most people on the planet aspire.

I tell Yahia this has been a special end to a rare week. Next week I'll be back with the children. I have taught three of Yahia's children, knew them well before I'd met Yahia or heard his poetry or the story of his life.

In Iraq, Yahia had been a teacher too – and a journalist – but lost accreditation when he refused to pledge allegiance to Saddam and the Baath Party. Under torture he signed an "agreement" that he would cease to criticise the regime. After release he continued to speak out knowing his name would now automatically be on the death-list. He left his family immediately and crossed the border. Later his wife Wejdan walked across the desert for three days with their children Shayma and Ali. They sought refuge in Saudi Arabia before making their way quietly to Australia.

Yahia tells me his later daughter Najed is named after the city in his homeland.

The name of his youngest, Sarah, means simply "Joy".

Yahia is still widely remembered and regarded in the Middle East for his poetic imagery and opposition to both the privileged excesses of the Shahs and the brutal dictatorship of Saddam

Hussein. His poetry in Arabic has won him the prestigious Prize of the Arab Union for Poetic Creativity. He continues to travel back for guest appearances at Writers' Festivals. He has published 15 volumes of poetry in Arabic and one in English.

Now Saddam is in prison. Yahia is free. Iraq is being torn apart after its 'liberation'.

But as Yahia says in verse:

> *"Leave my sacrificed country*
> *The slain people*
> *Orchards …*
> *Waterways … and clay*
> *And leave us in peace.*
> *We won't exchange the pig for the wolf..."**

Nothing will silence Yahia Al-Samawy.

And I am left with the faintest hope that perhaps the pen really can overcome the sword…

* excerpt from *Leave My Country* in *Two Banks with No Bridge* by Picaro Press, 2005. © Yahia al-Samawy, 2005. © English Translation Eva Sallis, 2005.

The bird leaves
its cage and
enters another

*for Juan Garrido-Salgado**

1990.
english was in the air.
the air
was english

blowing on a sea breeze at henley or glenelg
one sentence floats near you

but it will not come
into your mouth

tortured   barred
in & from   your homeland

mute in the newland
your heart bleeds metaphors
exiled from your tongue

alien vowels / consonants
fill your ears
elude your mouth

your heart an injured bird
one wing
plastered to tarmac

        an impotent flapping

                in spanish

* In 1990, Juan was granted asylum in Australia after fleeing Chile's Pinochet régime which burned his poetry, and imprisoned and tortured him.

A Clarity of Smog

nine days in Japan and already you're a megalomaniac
drunk on the fame of being slightly apart
backhome there are bushfires and The Test on TV but here
you're in the manic phase of a bipolar New Year.

even getting off the train at the wrong station when you can't
read the signage and no-one speaks your mother tongue doesn't
phase you. a divine messenger disguised as a mid-level clerk
tells you that the train to Mega is *nexto-nexto.*

you're completely alone in your ipod universe as Antony sings
everything is new in the space between your ears and you walk
the winter grey concrete streets of Mega / Shikama houses and
steel smokestacks beside a river tamed with cement.

refinery pipes, mega-pylons supporting arcs of cable
inscribed from some point above and
triangulations of scaffolding infrastructure
your artificial horizon.

you know in your bones that the sun rising red through smog
is rising just for you and despite the photochemical haze
there's a clarity   like individual rainbow ice crystals
refulgent on dead rice stalks beneath your feet.

the day is new. those birds you pass have migrated from Siberia
to forage for insects between the backstreet cabbages at this
precise second for your entertainment alone. you love each
moment.   like now.   and this one   now.

the entire day is unfolding. you don't need a god
when the Universe is so perfect and self-organised.
each day dripping into the vast pool
of days spent.

occasionally we find ourselves
at an intersection where
any choice will be
the right one.

Your Life ©

'Take me with you,' she said. 'I'll try harder, I promise.'

Those intense blue eyes he'd known since childhood. The same eyes watched over him as a shy boy. But now that young mother was frail and tentative and the skin that surrounded those sky-blue eyes was like a chamois left out in the sun...

He sighed deeply. The next few minutes would be pivotal.

Blow it and she'll never trust me again.

'It's not about trying harder, mum. The Lady from the Assessment Panel said your home was *borderline hygienic.* Last month's fall scared me too.'

Graham spoke softly. He paused for effect.

Rube considered each word in silence.

'Besides, taking you is out of the question. The Residency Grant gives me six months in the Rome studio. No mothers included. They won't offer it again.'

She continued the scrutiny.

Graham changed tack.

'Look. No-one's saying it's your fault... Your eyesight isn't what it was and it's hard to see dirt in corners and food left on dishes. In the Retirement Village you'd never have to wash another thing.'

Graham had mentally rehearsed. Avoid 'Nursing Home.' Stick with the straight-forward 'Retirement Village'. When he'd earlier mentioned 'Integrated Lifestyle Options', Rube had exploded 'New Age Bullshit! Why can't they call a spade a bloody shovel?'

In middle-age she'd be 'cantankerous.' Octogenarians are 'feisty'…

An overweight forty-something woman in a too-tight uniform gushed 'Welcome Ruby!' We've been expecting you for Special Visiting Day!'

The logo on her very ample left breast declared: 'Your Life ©. Your Choice.'

Pity. They can't write. In sentences…

'Just in time for Morning Tea!'
A ridiculously-cheerful girl was dispensing cups of tea from a décor-matched brushed-stainless trolley. The curtains were floral pinks, salmon and grey – the same fabric covering sofas and chairs. Even stainless-framed prints of peaceful forests and tranquil seas on clean walls echoed the shades in the furnishings. Everything was perfect. There were no fluff-balls in the corners of the Dining Room's vinyl floor or the Morning Room's carpet.

'Ruby! We've organised a Day Buddy for you!'

Jesus Christ.

Logo-Lady became old-school Kindy teacher, emphasising each syllable.

Does this woman think I'm deaf or stupid?

The Day Buddy, Barbara, meant well. The sort a teacher would pick to show you around on your first day.

It seemed that Your Life ©. was the answer to all Barb's prayers. Like Heaven without having to die.

Everything was done for you. The meals were nutritious and always on time. You could watch any programmes you liked in your own room (although, during the day Rube noted that Ridiculously Cheerful skipped over to the plasma screen and quickly switched from the News to an inane game-show.)

Perhaps they're trying to protect the old dears from upsetting events in the Outside World. I wonder how they'd handle my story about the ASIO goons breaking into my flat in the sixties. I'll bet none of the other ladies in here has a dossier on themselves. But they probably weren't members of the Australian Communist Party or agitated in Moratoriums either.

There is no up   water pressing in from all sides   her limbs powerless in the cotton nightdress   kelp in a storm   the compulsion to breathe in the sea, the will to fight it   then the swirling light beckoning   flailing, frogkicking towards the up she's found   grunting because she can't scream, struggling for a surface she can't reach   before lungs explode or water rushes in and takes her down   down down down to the deepest dark   she can't do it   her determination sickens, as her body will soon follow   her mouth opens inhaling salt water and the legs give one final spasm   she hears a distant scream. it is her own.

She is sitting up, rigid in a bed in a small room. The clock radio glows 2:47 in red. Her nightie is sweat-drenched, her heart fast and strong.

She has a one minute shower and puts on a fresh pair of flannelette pyjamas, turns on the kettle, gets out the cup and teabag.

The same dream that recurred all those years ago when ASIO were after me. It wasn't easy being a commo in 1950s Australia. Not that being in the Party was against the law although it would've been if Pig-iron Menzies had got his way. "Liberal". What a joke. But those ASIO blokes didn't have to worry about The Law. The distant clicks on the phone line as the unseen third listener connected. The non-descript goon in unfashionable suit who appeared half a block behind me whenever I'd arranged a meeting in town. The visits and questioning that always began with the loud rap on the front door just after I'd fallen asleep. It was psychological warfare. But I was always in control. Never let the bastards beat me.

The whistle of the old kettle interrupts her thoughts. *Like cutting to a new scene in a Hitchcock movie. A woman's scream transformed to a steam train shrieking out of a tunnel...*

I wonder if it was all worth it. My idealism vanished later after Hungary and Czechoslovakia. We still had to fight that referendum though... If Menzies had won that one we'd all be livin' under fascism. No room for dissent. But there were other causes. Ban the Bomb. The Women's Movement. The Environment. Hope the young people keep carryin' the torch. Seemed like they were only interested in 'emselves for a while. Turnin' green now but...

She knows now what she'll tell Graham.

59

Graham's positivity is rehearsed and irritating.

'Beautiful morning, Mum.'

She nods.

'Well. Did you sleep on it?'

Rube's response is equally rehearsed.

'Yep. You're prob'ly right… I'll pack me bags now if you like. It's all for the best. Less worry for you in Italy, too.'

'Yeah, well… no rush… But we can do it today if you like.'

Graham is pleased. Talking her around had been much easier than he'd expected. Still… it must be terrible being so independent for your whole life, then not really knowing what's best for you at the end.

Rube packs her bags. She doesn't even turn around for one last look before leaving. They'll probably nose through her few belongings on admission to Your Life ©.

She'll sneak back later by taxi for the 100mL bottle of Nembutal.

Still in full control.

She brushes a wisp of grey hair from her eyes with an arthritic hand and smiles.

Your Life. Your Choice.

mr miles

this morning out of the blue(s) i woke humming mr miles by
kurt elling a vocal version of a wayne shorter solo and then i
began wandering the backstreets of Himeji and Mega in my
mind because that's the association the wrong soundtrack to the
wrong movie way it always is wrong because when i was living
in japan i would always wear the headphones when walking
with the ipod in the top pocket so later in the day theres a very
ordinary old man buying fruit and veg at the hub or changing a
book at the library and no one knows why hes smiling with a
head full of jazz and scenes of gnarled wisteria blooming on
local shrines and kids riding past singsonging ohayogozaimasu
Rob-san, walking past an old man watering vegetables   under
an ancient stone torii wondering why this old man is humming
to himself   and smiling

up here on swanston

above kfc maccas and hungry jacks
persists an older melbourne.

above the cathedral arcade outside
collected works it's still the 1800s.

everyone's slower.   a shop
that only sells buttons.

winter sun draws oblique golden lines
through leadlight arches.

down the road at fedsquare a toddler
ignores thousands around him,

lost in tunnel vision joy. chasing
his shadow pixellating
on cobbles.

sees past thousands rushing about their
petty business, hubs of their own multiverses

while i worry about the rise of trump & hanson,
the fall of community,

the toddler   revels
in his own   moment.

Lost in trainstation

I have been listening to the train-driver for the name of my station, Shirahama. I've forgotten how many stops it is from Himeji. The station names come up in his unintelligible spiel as little lifeboats in a sea of incomprehension. Blah blah blah shikama blah blah blah mega blah blah blah...

It must be soon. I look outside, industrial mixed with domestic, and it all begins to have a déjà-vu feel. I know the school is close because of the smoke and steam pouring out of the smoke stacks I see in the distance every day from my other school. I haven't found out yet whether they belong to the Mitsubishi Paper Mill or a power station, but it seems we're not close enough yet.

We seem to be taking longer than last time... Surely we've stopped too many times? The station names are a purée of *hiragana*, *katakana* and *kanji* – none of which I can read any way. Some stations have a small English translation underneath in orange. I recognise the *Higashi-* and *Nishi-* prefixes before the place-names, but East and West what?

A panic begins to rise in me. *Befu*. I'm sure I've never been this far before. I ask around me *Sumimasen – Does anyone speak English here? Where is Shirahama?* Dozens of people smile at me sympathetically, but it's obvious that their English is as non-existent as my Japanese. I look at my watch. I've been on the train an hour! I should have been at the right stop by 8:00. It's now 8:30. I jump off the train at the next station. The other commuters disperse purposefully in their own confident directions. The rush, the groans and squeals of the train fade into the distance.

I am standing on the empty platform. Suddenly I am the guy in the movie who finds himself alone at the station in the middle of the prairie. But there are no tumbleweeds.

I'll ask a stationmaster how far back to Shirahama. No stationmaster.

In fact, no railway employees at all. It's just me and traintracks meeting at Vanishing Point on the Horizon in both directions, like some Year 8 Technical Drawing class...

At this station there are two machines covered in Japanese writing. One is a Fare Dispenser, the other Fare Adjustment. You can travel further than your ticket allows in Japan by making the appropriate adjustment when you arrive at your destination. Very civilised. There is also a huge amount of Japanese signage and one small sign which announces that I am at *Fuji-e*. It seems to be close to an industrial port, but the silence is deafening.

And then my saviour arrives. A well-dressed woman, perfectly coiffured, approaches. Er ... *Ohayo gozaimasu... sumimasen...* do you speak English? *Chotto*, she says, finger and thumb indicating that she has about one centimetre of English. *Shirahama?* She looks surprised, says "long way", pointing back to where I have come from. She looks surprised, but she is decisive. *Come.* She takes me to a small loudspeaker in a wall and pushes the button. She explains my predicament in rapid Japanese to the disembodied voice, then says *hai hai hai hai hai* and looks at me. *No plobrem. Next train one minutes.*

Count juku. Stations? I do a quick calculation. *Ju*, ten. *Ku*, nine. "Nineteen?" I nod and thank her profusely. It's probably not kosher Japanese mores, but I grab her hand and pump vigorously. The train is coming and I have to run fifty metres away from the station to a level crossing, then back up the ramp to the platform on the opposite side. No train stops at a station for longer than 30 seconds.

What did she mean by the nineteen? I can't possibly have gone 19 stops too far? Does she mean go back to station 19 or nineteen kilometres? There's no time for interrogation as my train arrives and my Good Samaritan (who's probably Buddhist) gives me the thumbs up from the opposite platform and I retrace my journey.

I picture my cell phone at home being uselessly recharged next to my bed. I can't contact my school to explain my lateness. By nine the first lesson has already begun, minus the stupid *gaijin* foreigner. Then a strange calm overcomes me. I realize I can't make the train go any faster. My school is probably ringing the Emergency Rooms of the major Himeji hospitals or the Education Board to ask them to transfer the Lemon Language Teacher to another school, but it's all out of my hands. I change from a paranoid ganglion of exposed raw neurons to a practising Zen monk. I almost enjoy the return journey.

And Shirahama is exactly where it should be (except that the station is called Shirahamanomiya, which, when spoken rapidly, as it invariably is, sounds nothing like Shirahama and doesn't look much like it on a sign blurring past at Mach-1.)

I run from the train and I'm amazed the machine accepts my Y290 ticket, not realising that I've probably just had thousands of Yen's worth of free travel freeloading off the Sanyo Line for the past two hours. I run the last few hundred metres to school, mentally preparing my apology with lots of broken Japanese and humble bows.

But when I arrive, school has been locked. Like a prison, the heavy gates have been wheeled across and padlocked. I spend a further ten minutes encircling the compound looking for a chink in the defences, but there isn't one. Eventually I find a lower part of the fence (under 5 feet), throw my backpack over and jump in. I only hope that no-one sees me and rings the police to say some big-nosed alien paedophile has just broken into the local elementary school...

But the practised apologies aren't required. The principal and teachers are just happy to see I'm safe and even happier to hear the story of the stupid *gaijin* who can't even catch a train without getting lost.

All morning a few white dinghies of words keep bobbing up in the sea of confusion. *Ju-ku!?* (Nineteen?!) *Wa? Ne?* followed by peals of hysterical laughter.

Border dispute

'Oh, hello, Marjorie. I didn't see you there.'

It was an absurd comment, really. If Em hadn't seen Marj she wouldn't be talking to her now. In any case, Marj had noticed Em through the venetians before stepping into the backyard with a plastic basket of wet washing. Em had been watering the same patch of lawn by hand-held hose for at least ten minutes. She must have been lying in wait.

If Marj knew anything about Emily Watkins, it was that she was a small-minded busy-body. Perhaps her nose was out of joint because she hadn't been invited to last night's little soirée and she was looking for something to whinge about...

Marj wasn't about to become victim. She'd grab the bull by the horns. Make the first move. Stay in charge.

'Good morning, Mrs Watkins. Your lawn's looking nice.' *And so it should if all of it gets the attention that this square metre has had for the past ten minutes.*

'Er... Thankyou Mrs Pilkington.' Marj had already deflated her sails.

'I hope the noise from my party didn't disturb you last night. Some of those chaps from The Club can get a bit rowdy when they're a bit shickered.'

Emily Watkins took a sharp breath, her cheeks already flushed in anticipation of what she'd been rehearsing since 11:30 pm. It just wasn't on.

The Covenant said expressly

> *Residents will not entertain guests or*
> *make excessive noise after*
> *• 10 pm on a weeknight or*
> *• midnight on a Saturday.*

Friday night was clearly a weeknight. Rules was rules. They was not made for some people and not others. Start making exceptions and you're on the Slippery Slope and before you can say Permissive Generation, the whole of Society has gone down the toilet. And as for using bad language like *shickered*, Marjorie Pilkington should know better. Goodness knows what those drunkards from the Glandore Bowling Club got up to. And her, widowed for less than two years. She should of known better.

'Actually, since you mentioned it, Mrs Pilkington,' Emily sniffed, 'there was an access of noise yesterday evening. Clearly beyond the pale.'

'I'm sorry that you...' Marj began, but she was not to finish.

'Bad enough last Thursday with Mrs Fisk Up The End... there's only so much I'll put up with... you should of been ashamed of yourself carrying on. All those single men and laughing at the top of your voice on a week-night... oh, it's all right for some. Some of us've got to get up early on Saturday for the Auxiliary Roster. I've bitten my tongue for far too long, the Body Corporate will hear about this and you'll be out of here before you can say The Lord's Prayer not that you prob'ly ever have. Rules is Rules.'

Clearly an apology was a waste of time. Marj took a deep breath and peered into Emily Watkins' red face.

'All right, Em. You win. Let's go to the Residents' Meeting together. I'll give them all the details about how you water your lawn in the middle of the day during Level 3 Water Restrictions. They take a very dim view of that. Rules are Rules, after all.'

For the first time in her life Emily Watkins was stuck for words. At the mention of 'Water Restrictions' she went into cardiac arrest – an arrest from which, sadly, she never recovered.

It was a small funeral. Marj Pilkington wore her best dress and pearls. She sat in the tiny chapel almost alone, save for a couple of employees of the funeral parlour and a young girl from Meals on Wheels. Emily Watkins had never married. There were no relatives and she'd never made many friends.

So sad, Marj thought to herself. *If only she'd been a little more tolerant she could have enjoyed her last years...*

At the graveside it began to rain. Marj produced a grim smile.

By the end of the month Water Restrictions had been rescinded.

Roly Poly Pudding

I.

At life's end there's a simplification, the man divests of
Possessions   his family moves on

he leaves his wife   and his life
contracts   to this tiny shack.

The man becomes boy;
boy, baby.

The day is hot in his two rooms of asbestos
neither the air nor the tide moves

he sits on a kitchen chair before a single
electric fan, talkback
his only company.

Refuses to buy an airconditioner.
Spends the morning bathed in sweat
watching the sea.

Waiting for the breeze
that comes with the afternoon
tide.

Dressed only in his incontinence nappy
Life has become eating   sleeping
pissing   shitting.

The district nurse visits daily now
in loco parentis tells him
to look after the diabetes.

She leaves. He drinks lemonade,
cons neighbours through guile
to buy him cakes   cream & sticky buns.

The girl from the bakery comes daily
but won't enter the shack, repelled by the diaper,
the fetid odour and rolypoly rolls of fat.

He survives. remembering from his business in the seventies
how to manipulate others

From pity, fishermen give him
whiting, gar, tommies, crabs.
he accepts the fish   rejects the friendship

It's all been stripped away.
He won't touch the money in the bank
severs bonds and obligations of relationship,
wallows in selfpity, self destruction. filth.

II.

Now he's moving into the Home where he can sit in a modern sofa
in surroundings fashionably sterile. Sits and watches the same sea,
further up the coast

The date for the auction's been set.

His wife's son takes what he needs, leaves the shed door open.
Retirees help themselves   to fishing tackle   rusted tools
his possessions dispersed, reabsorbed into nearby
sheds, the dispersal of The Estate
preceding his
passing

Cigarette

Watanabe stares at his fingers curled round the steering wheel. Other teachers see him in the carpark as they arrive. Perhaps he's planning the day's lessons or waiting for the end of the news. But when he isn't in the staff room 30 minutes later they go back and there he is, staring through the windscreen. Seeing nothing. When they knock on his window he says he's fine, grabs his collapsed briefcase and heads for the office.

Perhaps the hacking cough will be eased by a cigarette. Morning Staff Meeting has finished early. He can get down to the ground floor, slip on his Outside Shoes and hide behind the gate pillar for a quick draw – maybe three quarters of a Hope – and back to Lesson 1 in four minutes. He's done it before. He gives a nod or a '-*masu*'.

There's a small knot of them there. All middle-aged men with grey hair and skin to match. The students are safely locked in. Only late-arrivals will see their teachers drinking in the furtive smoke. *Nomimasu*. Drinking. The chrome gate is a massive structure on track and wheels. It could keep out a tank.

All the men dye their hair. Some try to take off twenty years and go for black, but most go for a shade somewhere between. Like that *gaijin* book, he thinks grimly, fifty shades of grey. At least he doesn't have one of those cheap jobs with their tinge of purple or blue…

The public address plays the Chimes of Dunkirk and they draw in deep, final inhalations and the glowing orange tips race towards their lips. They squint from smoke and concentration or pleasure and stamp out unfinished butts and the nicotine is already in the bloodstream for the three hour haul until lunchtime.

Watanabe's hands shake. He was called out by the police this morning at 2 a.m. Some kids in his class were causing trouble at the 24 hour McDonalds. The police always call the *sensei* first. There were no charges pressed. A brow-beating for the boys from him, *gomenasais* all round to Manager and Police, then drive the boys home to their parents. All this in less than two hours, but at home he couldn't get back to sleep. If his wife were still there he could talk to her. Perhaps she would massage his shoulders. She'd been good at that. Now she was back with her parents. The chances of reconciliation were about as likely as snow in July and neither wanted the shame of divorce.

At four he takes the last temazepam he begged from the doctor. It doesn't work, his mind a spinning roulette wheel. The little silver ball of thoughts spins against the wheel, rolls down into a groove and whips into a circle. Then it jumps out *Pachinko!* bounces off the rim like a pinball and flies off at a new tangent.

Will she ever come back? I must submit my schedule tomorrow morning... I forget return-gift for Sakata-sensei... three more math tests to correct before Thursday... should I get my hair cut before parent interviews?

He turns the light back on. Perhaps one more cigarette.

And so it goes, one thought bouncing off another like a pachinko ball, each tangent a catalyst for a new chain reaction. Yes. He is the pachinko ball. Contained. Out of control.

A house of cards

His name means Light. When he smiles the sun shines.
He is screaming because the door is usually open.
Today it is closed.

His autism blows storms from unexpected directions.
He attempts something new. Another child's comment.
A routine is changed.

The flimsy edifice of his confidence is raised, razed.
Even the worst tempest abates.
His screams subside.

Each day his teacher steadies his hand, helps
him to reconstruct the house of cards
named resilience.

crabbing from james well to rogues point

a lowtide worm pumps its way through slush of sand to leave a rounded mound with a breathing hole, a micro shield volcano. this repeated infinitely so the whole beach is a wet moonscape glinting in morning sun

we eke out food, the birds and i. slow-wading with an occasional darting lunge. rare catches between frequent misses   a kind of purposeful tai chi, slomo meditation. today i share the point with cormorants drying wings, fossicking oystercatchers and chats and not-turning terns. working my way to the rocky point i know they won't allow me proximity, last moment flapping up circling long arcs to return to the same rocky point after my passing

thighdeep water in seagrass a splash just behind two shiny black fins withdraw into becalmed water like twin baby dolphins swimming side by side as the tips submerge a third vertex of the unseen triangle a barb emerges behind in a heart-thump an image of Steve Irwin's chest leaps to mind but my movements are slow, deliberate for five minutes stingray and human warily circle each other going about the business of hunting crabs, predators keeping a wide berth respecting each other's borders in this slow mundane ballet

Through a glass, darkly

Of course I first became aware last night that the piece was missing.

Some might say that I am obsessive. Perhaps they are correct. I am always pleased to share my passion for collecting, but I like to see everything returned to its proper place before retiring. I sent my housekeeper off to bed.

It was then that I realised the Burmese Blue was missing. It is a small piece, my first and I'm particularly fond of it, having acquired it in Rangoon, more than thirty years ago. It was the birth of my interest in the beauty of Burmese glass, and Melodie would have known this, but I'll deal with her later.

I scoured the carpet in my Collection Room, checked behind sofas, lifted cushions and so forth – all to no avail. I was still convinced that it had merely been misplaced, you see. When I found myself repeatedly looking in places I knew I'd checked previously, I became frantic and checked the upstairs rooms. After a sleepless night I determined to notify the Police at a more respectable hour in the morning.

I was up early, busying myself with tidying the house, hard work and routine being something of a comfort for me.

Downstairs, on the duvet in the Guest Room, was a handbag. I couldn't remember whose it was. I opened it and there was Melodie's driver's licence, just loose in the bag. Typical Melodie – she's such a flibbertijibbet, I thought – her Louis Vuitton had special compartments for licences, but here it was, just thrown in with her lipsticks, compact and nail-file. Then I saw the sparkle of blue.

At that moment it all became clear. My best friend was a thief.

It was as if someone had hit me from behind with a club. I actually reeled forward in shock and had to sit on the bed.

Suddenly I realized I had never really trusted Melodie, with her girlish name and her sing-song voice to match.

We'd had a kind of sororal relationship vacillating between love and hatred. We'd become close at College. She was the party-girl; I was the more reserved. Perhaps she was a little jealous of me. I studied harder and achieved the better grades. It was me, Dorothy Blunt, who steadfastly and persistently built up a portfolio of clients who appreciated my conservative approach to financial management. I'd acquired this substantial home in Adelaide and filled it with beautiful objets d'Art.

Certainly Melodie had the good looks and wasn't averse to flaunting her slim figure at all and sundry.

I've always suspected her of stealing William, my one and only fiancé who just moved to another city one day without having the intestinal fortitude to face me. William and his cowardly two-page letter… Oh, I know he didn't run off with Melodie, but it was she with her loose morals who'd set his eye to straying. Just as she batted those cheap false eyelashes at Neville last night before accepting his lift home. No self-control,

Melodie. Can't even steal without making a complete shen-
nanigans. Robs me on impulse, drinks like a dipsomaniac,
forgets her bag and allows the first man who asks her to drive
her home. I have no doubt Neville had his way with the little
strumpet. If she were here now I'd be tempted to bring one of
my pieces down on her thin skull, crack! like an almond shell...

However, unlike Melodie Tripp, I have morals. I shall ring
the local police and report the theft. Later, in their presence, I
shall discover the glass in her ostentatious Louis Vuitton and put
on a show of histrionics. She will be met by the full force of the
Law.

Melodie may not look quite so pretty in prison garb.

I may even show some Christian charity and visit her in gaol...

watching the firebombing

Its very ordinariness is frightening. You've seen the American footage countless times. The opening of the bomb-bays on Dakotas or B52s. Bombs dropping like clouds of confetti on nameless factories and cities below. First fat drops of rain onto dust. Little puffs billowing.

You see an image of Himeji Castle and in the Japanese commentary hear the word Tegara – the suburb you're in at this moment – and realise that on July 3rd, 1945 (the eve of US Independence Day), those bombs were raining down right here.

And the few survivors who are still alive in this millennium tell how in one two-hour raid, those bombers dropped their deadly cargo in a broad band from Himeji Port to Kodera and 713 died and 10,000 were injured.

And sixty-three years on, these old men and women still break down when they describe the bombs which were designed to explode into miniature fireballs to burn wooden houses and the flesh of women and children because there were few men left. Bodies burnt so black they looked like fallen charcoal statues.

You feel that familiar sense of futility and realise that war doesn't discriminate between soldier and civilian, between guilty and innocent. You wonder at the 'enlightened' decision of Macarthur and Roosevelt to spare culturally and historically 'significant' structures like Himeji Castle and most of Kyoto and only incinerate expendable humans.

Two weeks earlier they'd bombed the 'legitimate' military target of a fighter-plane factory in Kyoguchi. But now the target was a band of civilians a kilometre wide and fifteen long. At 10pm the Tegara Elementary School was flattened, with no one inside. But many of its students, at home nearby on their *tatami* mats and *futons*, died anyway.

It is a day like any other. The sounds of birds drift in through open summer windows, along with the roar of a motorbike deliberately revving past the school. A *shinkansen* that doesn't stop in Himeji rumbles past at breakneck speed across the six-storey overpass.

The students are unusually quiet. A few studious ones take notes. The boy at the back with the long spiky hair has lost interest and is passing notes to another boy. This black-and-white video is history. He hates history. Sixty years may as well be six hundred or six thousand. These people lived well before he was born – or his parents.

It's not his experience. I hope it never will be. His apathy doesn't upset me. I'm glad he lives in a society that tolerates a little rebellion. He won't be beaten for his spiky hair. He won't be shot for his defiant pink hair-clip.

At the end of the video the teacher tells the quietened thirteen-year-olds that when she was a student in Hiroshima she heard many first-hand eye-witness accounts of the Bomb and the War.

'Now those people's experience has died with them, but we must never forget. And no matter how depressed we may get, we should reject suicide.   For life is precious.'

cold caller

I had a funny phone call the other day.

He said you don't know me I'd like a few minutes of your time.

I'm not trying to sell you anything. Just give me two minutes, ok ?

I thought what the hell.

He said we've never met but I've been interested in your work for years. I let him go on...

Perhaps it was the flattery

I'd had a lot of rejections recently.

He mentioned something I'd performed years ago before a small audience in another city.

How could you know about that ?

I asked

I know everything about you   your career your personal life your most intimate thoughts

Hey who is this?

I told you.   You don't know me.   Remember when you were in hospital a few years back? I wanted to visit you but they wouldn't let me.

Now this guy on the phone was really irritating me.

Yet I was curious and I wanted to know more.

Can we meet? It slipped out before I'd really considered the implications.

You don't want that he said.

We can never meet. You can't see my face. At least you can—
but only once.   We've never met but you know me.

My name is death.   Just the one name.   I have no family.   I
have no friends.   I just wanted to touch base. We'll chat quite a
lot over the next few years and one day   we'll meet.
Take care.

Mr Vanehouse

Someone pulled the chain on the big brass school bell and we all filed in and sat at the cast-iron K-frame desks. You had to lower the hinged bench seat slowly because, first, Mr Vanehouse didn't like the clatter, and second, you'd spatter the Quink out of the little white porcelain ink wells, which looked like upside down Dutch caps, which was pretty funny because Mr Frank Vanehouse was actually Dutch.

"Good morning everyvon," he said, and we chanted a reply.

You could tell he was in a good mood today. This meant we might be able to distract him later from the lesson with a question about The War. I liked his deep melodious voice. He could have been an American radio announcer except that his *th* sounds came out as *d*.

Cowandilla Demonstration School was a kind of model school in the 1960s. Some of us kids were Anglos but many were from families who'd come by boat from Europe – Greece, Italy, Poland, Germany, Cyprus, Malta and all the countries that Russia had invaded. It wasn't a wealthy area, but the teachers there had extra qualifications for giving demonstration lessons to student teachers from the nearby Western Teachers College. Mr Vanehouse had also taken on the New Maths, which was being trialled in the school by an eccentric Hungarian Professor of Maths and Psychology called Zoltan P. Dienes. I loved it. Venn diagrams and algebra, negative numbers and "maths equipment" and graphing equations in Grade 6. And working in pairs and groups from activities on cards and progressing at our own rate – quite an innovation in 1964!

After about an hour of Maths, Mr Vanehouse told us to pack up the gear and we settled down for one of his stories.

"Who vould have t'ought dat I'd end up teaching mademadics?!" he said, as if he were talking to a group of adults.

After the first few weeks we didn't notice his accent. It was just part of who Mr Vanehouse was.

"On my last day of high school in Holland my Professor sat next to me on da tram. He said 'good luck for da vuture, yong man. You might make a good teacher von day yourselv. But stay avay from mademadics – you only just parsed dat von!'"

I liked the way Mr Vanehouse told these human stories. It made up for the times he'd get angry – he had a very short fuse and he'd roar at a kid who was defiant and chuck him out of the classroom. Sometimes, for good measure, as he left the room he would give him a kick up the arse.

He'd make sarcastic comments about the Germans and the Poles as if oblivious to the German and Polish kids in the class. One morning I began to understand this resentment and anger boiling just below the surface. He was walking across the playground and saw me parking my treadly in the bike racks.

"Nice bike, Robert," he said, drawing in smoke.

The two fingers holding the cigarette were pushed up to expose his two bad front teeth and the gap between them. The smoke magically went uphill from his mouth into his nose like a blurry waterfall in reverse. He once confided to the whole class about the bad teeth. Under German occupation they didn't get much good food – mostly watery soup – and the vitamin and mineral deficiency while his teeth were developing meant that now his deformed teeth looked like a dirty broken picket fence.

But here he was today admiring my bike. It wasn't an especially flash one. Dad didn't make that much money as a cabinetmaker in those days, so the bike was a restored second-hand birthday present. It was still my pride and joy. Mr Vanehouse looked admiringly at the two-wheeler, and his mind travelled 10,000 miles to another hemisphere and backwards in time twenty years.

"I godda bike for my birthday too," he said.

It was more like he was speaking to my bike than me.

"I vos riding it for da virst time wid my mate. Ve should have been smarder... Da vor vasn't going well vor da Germans. Dey were calling up old men and boys, confiscading any form of transport. Da soldier saw us and yelled ad us to stop. Ve wheeled our bikes over to da checkpoint. He checked our papers. He vent bag in to speak to his boss. Ve looked ad each odder, den jumped on our bikes and pedalled as vast as our skinny legs vould take us. A vhistle blew. Ve pushed harder. Dere was a crack! and a bullet vhistled past my left ear... I'll never vorget dat zound."

Mr Vanehouse had pulled his head down into his worn tweed jacket and was hunching his shoulders as if that bullet was still whistling past his left ear. I didn't know what to say. I've thought many times since of all the questions I might have asked him. But I just stood there by the bike racks, a grade six boy in shorts. Dumb.

"Ve had von secont to decide vedder to turn arount," Mr Vanehouse said. "Dere was no question. Your life is wert more dan a bike. Ve handed dem over. I'd had da bike von day. I never saw it again."

91

The New Disappearers

It was the homeless who began to disappear at first. No one noticed. They lived on the fringes and their non-existence didn't impinge on anyone else's life. Just small pockets, by ones and twos, so that the Big Picture wasn't affected.

There was no violence involved. In the late seventies Los Desaparecidos were eliminated by a secret arm of the military state of Argentina. The Disappearers demise was more benign.

There was no satisfactory explanation. Scientists dismissed the incidents as "unsubstantiated and isolated reports", condemned the observers as "hysterical and New Age" and demanded that the government increase expenditure on science education.

Before long it was the aged and deinstitutionalized individuals with some form of disability or disease who faded away. The process was simple, if inexplicable. At first these people ceased to exist in the mass media. They didn't show up on social media, sitcoms or panel shows. They never made the news. Then came the more curious part. Initially they became a little less vivid – less depth-of-field, less colour. Then they became imperceptibly transparent or translucent. Just enough that you might just faintly see the pattern on the fabric of the seating behind or under them on a train or a bus. Or the writing on the billboard they walked in front of didn't entirely disappear. Soon their reflections in shop windows would become less distinct.

It began with the so-called marginalized but gradually extended to anyone who wasn't hugely popular – the overweight, the ugly, the less-than-average, who had been ignored by the media for years, so their actual disappearance wasn't problematic.

Curiously at the same time celebrities became brighter, more vivid, more intense. More life-like than life itself. Common people began to colour their hair and wear iridescent cosmetics to emulate their freakish heroes.

Andy Warhol's prediction that every one would get their fifteen minutes of fame never eventuated. Celebrity was concentrated on fewer people whose every move was closely studied by the commoners as they themselves paled away.

People became famous by virtue of being a celebrity, not by contributing anything worthwhile to humanity or the society which supported them. Fame came by being briefly associated with another celebrity or being on a quirky vidbyte which went viral.

After a few months there was only a small cohort of intense personalities (phosphorescently technicoloured, larger than life itself) who were noticed. Some of the paler people began capturing the images of the many-hued celebrities and selling them at grossly inflated fees to media outlets. Some of these image-gatherers themselves became famous by association.

Soon almost all of the Common People had faded to nothingness. The Brilliant Ones, as they'd come to call themselves had no skills to grow or prepare food, make or clean clothes or look after themselves at all, really.

Within a week or two of the final demise of The Average Ones, the Brilliant Ones simply starved to death.

They had had their fifteen minutes. In the future everyone will be anonymous for eternity.

Electrician

He was entering the MRI. Hearing the industrial ker-thunk ker-thunk. The MRI retreated and the pounding was inside his head.

Then he awoke and the pounding was pain.

The real MRI had happened last year after the car accident, just as a precaution. But where was he now?

He tried to put the pieces back together, but it wasn't easy. Doing a jigsaw with welding gloves, drunk.

Had he been drugged? The fog in his head was the one he'd had as a kid when the appendix came out. That sour metallic taste...

*   *   *

Somewhere near Tsumago, Amano was preparing "the subject" for questioning. He had no idea who the subject was or what his crimes were. It was better that way. It wasn't personal. This man had transgressed the Law, or he wouldn't be here. He may have lied or tried to steal from the organization. It didn't matter.

Amano's loyalty to the Yakuza was unquestioning.

Within two days this man will answer questions about anything. He will betray his own mother. He will plea for his life and scream like a woman.

The subject was stirring, the drugs wearing off.

Amano, simply "The Electrician" to the Family, laid out his cable-ties, pliers, screwdriver and electric drill. He was a professional. He could extract information as cleanly as a dentist pulls teeth. He was able to get a confession from any man in 24 to 36 hours using basic tradesman's tools. And at the end of the job, simply wash them in water and throw them in the back of his van and return to his other work in the city. He would create no more suspicion than any other worker in this country under constant construction.

He gripped the drill like a pistol and pulled the trigger. It was fully recharged, the speed set to 'steel' so it screamed like a premonition of the sounds that would soon be echoing off these walls.

He stared at the shortened little finger with pride. Yakuza often had the tip of a finger lopped off. It wasn't punishment – he had always been loyal to the group – but a means to prove his oneness with The Family. In the seventeenth century the *Kabukimono*, the antecedents of the modern Yakuza, removed small sections of fingers, knowing that it weakened the grip on the samurai sword. This reduced the individual's power and strength as a swordsman, but it also ensured his reliance on the group.

When the subject was fully conscious the Electrician would get to work. He removed his shirt revealing the *irezumi*. He always worked shirtless. The house would have to remain sealed while he was completing his work. Certainly, he wouldn't be sweating as much as the subject, but it was hot work. In any case he liked to display his full-body tattoos. Only Yakuza were privileged to wear *irezumi*, that intricately flowing body-art applied by hand, ink and bamboo skewer to create icons of tigers and dragons symbolising power, action and ruthlessness.

As a surgeon wears a gown, so The Electrician wasn't fully-dressed for work until he stripped to his bare skin.

Most tourists think of Japan as wall-to-wall city, but there is still some of the most rugged and beautiful wilderness on the planet on these islands. Even on the largest island, Honshu.

Tsumago was planted in this wilderness. A few tourists came to hike the old Edo Highway, the remnants of a four-foot-wide paved road which once carried foot traffic between Kyoto, the ancient capital, and Edo, now Tokyo. But at night the tourists went back to their cities or stayed in the *ryokan*, the traditional inns around Tsumago and Otsumago. None ventured to an old farmhouse in a secluded valley 12 miles away.

A man could scream here at night and no-one outside would ever hear.

A man would scream here tonight.

kenny's gun

kenny. dangerous. exciting. he had an older sister who brought home records and boyfriends. when his parents argued, his father would get the shits and storm off for whole weekends to shoot foxes and trap rabbits near eudunda. even bought kenny an air rifle when he was only ten, the year i got my first bike.

the first and last day i shot a gun.

bored with the dull clang of hitting baked bean cans. *c'mere*, said kenny. i did. we went through the hole in the rotting picket fence. *the old duck knows i come 'ere. dudn't mind. seen her yesdy arvo. lars weeken too.*

the whole backyard shaded by huge ancient almond trees. sparrows twittered high in branches. kenny's first shot had one quivering spastically in the underfoot leaf litter, flapping futile wings. the side of its head flat, matted, soft, darkly wet. one eye gone.

what'd ya do that for? i whispered, blinking away hot tears. the thrill, excitement and danger of kenny had evaporated.

the backyard silent but for tiny final spasms in dead leaves. then the bird, and perhaps the whole world, was silent. kenny was indignant.   *'smatter?*

It was only a bloody sparrow

The first day

Maybe Mrs Vick didn't explain.

Maybe I wasn't listening properly.

But suddenly all of the kids were standing and going out into the sunshine.

"Where are we going?" I whispered to the boy next to me.

"Recess."

"What's reassess?"

"It means we eat."

I had to make sure. It seemed that most of the other kids had been to kindy before the first day of school. I hadn't had this practice. I was trying very hard to get everything right.

I went to my brand-new schoolbag. It was the leather kind that no one seems to have anymore, with a strap so you could wear it slung across one shoulder or on your back. Dad had put a white dot of paint right in the middle of the flap so I wouldn't get it mixed up with anyone else's. I got out the peanut paste sandwich. I was certain I had the right bag and the right lunch. Mum had cut that sandwich into four identically neat squares and wrapped it in waxed paper. There might have been a piece of cake or fruit too, but I don't remember everything that happened in 1958.

Other kids were playing but I kept right on eating.

Then an ancient looking lady rang the biggest handbell I'd ever seen and we went back into our new classroom to learn about a and smell our new pure-white books.

Soon the bell rang again. Mrs Vick sat us on the floor on prickly mats and told us it was lunch-time. What was I to do? I'd eaten everything at the first break.

It wasn't that I was hungry.

I just wanted to do the right thing to please Mrs Vick.

Mrs Vick saw the tears welling in my brown eyes, put an arm around me and said

"Whatever's wrong, Robert?"

I told her that I didn't have anything left. (I also suddenly had an urgent need to wee but I was sure I could hang on.)

After she'd sent the class out to play Mrs Vick took my hand and led me to a place called Staff Room. She asked me to choose one biscuit from a plate and one piece of fruit. I chose an apple from a pretty china bowl on the laminex table in the middle of the room full of smiling ladies.

I smiled back and said thankyou.

It was only half way through day one and I was already beginning to fall in love with Mrs Vick.

Toppin' y'self

Can't be an easy thing, but.

Toppin' y'self, I mean… Y'know, suicide.

I was just a schoolkid, like, y'know. Little tacker. Playing with the Schomburgk kids in their backyard when we seen the ambulance pull up in Kitson Avenue. Yeah. "Avenue". Sposeta have trees aren't they? Like *Les Grands Avenues* in Paris. Tree-lined. I can't remember one fuckn tree in Kitson Avenue. Just tiny red-brick Housing Trust homes.

Ronnie lived there. His ol' man worked for Gilbarco makin' petrol pumps for service stations. Pretty funny he couldn't afford a car 'imself, eh? Neither did Wayne's old man next-door. He was as tall as he was skinny. We used to joke that he didn't need a ladder to be a linesman for the Electricity Trust, 'cause he could reach the wires anyway. Sometimes he'd spend all his pay of a Fridy night at the pub and we'd have to show him where he lived. The old memory wasn't so good on Friday nights…

But we didn't know who lived in the old light grey house. Chris said he thought they were New Australians.

When they brought him out on the stretcher you couldn't see him with the blue sheet over his face. Mrs Schomburgk said we couldn't go and watch, but she went down and when she came back she said he'd gassed himself. My grandpa had been

101

gassed in the First War with somethink called "mustard". That was why one of his lungs was collapsed. I was a bit confused how this could happen in a person's house in Richmond South Australia in the 1960s... Later, back home, Mum explained that he'd turned on the oven without lighting it and put his head in...

I couldn't imagine ever being that sad that you didn't want to wake up. When I was a kid, I mean.

They were fixing up Marion Road at the time – making it wide and modern. Tearing up the old tram tracks so they could fit more cars on, I guess. They put these giant steel water pipes under the road and a man went right in on his back on a kind of stretcher with wheels. And he had welding equitment to seal the seams. I almost shat meself as he disappeared, just fittin' in the pipe, like he was buryin' himself alive under the road. Like putting his head in an oven. But he kept coming out and going back in. I thought he was so brave.

When I was at high school, a cabinetmaker who worked with Dad shot himself in the mouth. The bullet went out the back of his head and he lived. When he was recoverin' dad told him you have to be so careful cleanin' guns... The bloke says "I wasn't cleaning it. I was tryin' to do meself in."

I felt sorry for the bastard. He wasn't a freak. But ya can't help but wonder what happens to a normal bloke...

Holding on

Nineteen seventy one. My first year of tertiary education. On the way home to Richmond from Western Teachers College. More hippy than trainee teacher. I stop at the second-hand shop at Hilton, park the burgundy Vespa. Remove the red-and-white crash helmet, let the hair fall to my shoulders and enter the musty rooms filled with old furniture I won't need for two years because I'm still living with my parents.

My eyes fall on a photo in a large frame. It's a crap photo but the frame is old and beautiful. Perhaps walnut. I buy it for two dollars. It somehow survives the slow scooter ride home between my knees.

Back home my brother Lindsay and I tear the brown paper off the back and remove the photo from the glass. This could frame Hendrix or the Woodstock poster!

Behind the photo is an exquisite charcoal drawing of an old man with a white beard. But what draws us in is not his facial hair – really just an absence of rendering – but the kindness of his eyes. Piercing eyes rendered in dark brown charcoal.

For two years the drawing lives on the masonite wall of the tiny sleepout Dad built for me when he lost his job in the late sixties.

In nineteen seventy three at the age of nineteen I marry my girlfriend Lyn. We both move straight from our parents' houses to live together in a cheap maisonette somewhere between our two childhood homes. Fresh start. I leave my coin collection and 'works of art' to my younger brother Lindsay. There are some things you have to let go. Linds, four years younger, appreciates art and photography. It's the only thing to do.

Lindsay marries Gail. They take with them the charcoal portrait they name "Matthew" which (who?) looks down on them in their Allenby Gardens bungalow for twenty years.

Matthew's kind eyes supervise the newlyweds, home renovations, the arrival home from hospital of two beautiful girls, Sarah and Alice. Matthew watches them learn to walk and talk, their milestones through kindy and school. Matthew's kind eyes look down when Linds first gets the blinding headache and the partial paralysis. They look on kindly after the diagnosis of gioblastoma, Lindsay's preparing to go to hospital and coming home after the operation when it is clear that nothing would stop this malignant tumor.

These eyes observe benignly on the day that Lindsay passes away at home and we come to see him in his own bed, peaceful and cold.

After the funeral when Dad and I are helping to clean out Lindsay's shed, Gail asks me to take anything I want. I take a few things.

I don't take the portrait.

Perhaps two years later, browsing in a second-hand shop on Port Road, Hindmarsh, during lunch break from some tedious teachers' conference, there it is. The eyes have grown even kinder over the years, though his face doesn't seem as old. The old man who is now a part of the fabric of my late younger brother's life. "Matthew" is still old, but I am catching up.

The proprietor catches me studying the face intently.

"Nice drawing," he says.

I nod. Don't even ask how much. Just turn and walk out of the shop.

Holding on. Letting go.

Civility

– a personal reflection on the nature of courtesy
and language in contemporary Japan

Something they never seem to consider in those quality-of-living surveys or 'the most liveable city' nominations is the notion of 'civility'. Maybe that's an old-fashioned word these days or perhaps there's a better word that eludes me but I'll try to elaborate.

We lived in Himeji, Japan, for all of 2008 and again in 2012. After the initial culture-shock of residing in a city where the vast majority didn't speak our native language, the thing which impressed us most was the level of courtesy to strangers. I guess this is the true test of manners. It's easy to be polite to the friends we choose or someone from whom we want something. Showing respect to a person you may never meet again is the purest form of civility. We saw examples of this genuine decency every day. Certainly crime was low. After a few weeks in Japan my money-belt was relegated to the bottom of the suitcase where it didn't see light again until we packed to leave. We walked through districts in strange towns at night and never felt the least bit unnerved.

But it was a much more pro-active civility than low crime stats. The wallet containing several thousand yen, my credit cards and ID fell out of my pocket in the main street of Himeji while I was running for a bus. I realized my loss when I began searching for loose change to pay the driver. Someone on the bus intervened and paid my fare. At the elementary school I was posted for the day I was urged to report it to the police immediately. My supervisor from the Himeji Board of Education came to collect me and act as interpreter. I was given time off school so it could be done immediately. Several days later my completely-intact wallet was given back to me by the police. They had no reservations about giving me the name and address of the factory worker who'd handed it in. I went to visit him in his small apartment and eventually convinced him to accept a reward. Through my Japanese work-colleague, volunteering as translator, my savior explained that he didn't feel comfortable about accepting the money as it was 'simply the right thing to do.' It took some persuasion to get him to accept a token of appreciation for his honesty and time.

Even with our extremely limited grasp of Japanese we had no compunction about travelling anywhere in that amazing country because we knew that if we had a problem there would be some kind person somewhere to offer help. We only had to consult a map outside a train station and people would come up to ask if we were lost. On our first day in Osaka we wanted to see the amazing Sky Building but our Lonely Planet directions seemed to be wrong. (We later discovered they weren't – we'd confused Osaka Station with Shin-Osaka.) The owner of a small café / bakery was having trouble explaining the way to us. Then she said "You come," asked a neighbouring shop owner to watch her small business and walked us two blocks until we could see our destination towering over the cityscape.

We saw these small acts of kindness every day. Teens on public transport were chatty and exuberant like adolescents anywhere but there was no pushing and shoving, no surliness or outright meanness.

I'm sure a lot of people in Australia think I'm a bit of an old fuddyduddy primary school teacher when I start banging on about the decline of manners. But to me it's the oil in the machine called civil society. You can withhold the oil for a little while without obvious effect but eventually, without respect for strangers, the whole superstructure grinds to a halt or flies apart.

We returned to Adelaide from the beginning of 09 and I've given the Japanese question a lot of thought since then. I'm not saying Japanese society is perfect (they have organised crime and murder like any society although a lot of it seems to be related to drugs and the mafia-like Yakuza). Random violent attacks are exceptionally rare.

It may be that the long stable history of the country contributes to a kind of peace and sense of place (notwithstanding the expansionism of the 30s & 40s and two atom bombs!). It may be the strong Shinto and Buddhist traditions (although these bonds are weakening). I just don't know.

I accept that Himeji is a modest city (smaller even than my hometown of Adelaide) and my impression would have been quite different had I lived in Tokyo. And I wasn't wearing rose-coloured glasses either — I saw bad behaviour and fights in the Junior High where I worked — but the over-all impression was still one of a society where the common good was seen as an important priority and many decisions (by both teachers and students) were made by consensus rather than some blind obedience to authority.

I don't know what their secret is — but I'm sure we can all learn from them!

I'm quite certain that this whole civility thing was a determining factor when in 2011 we began considering another year's teaching in Japan. This time we'd be teaching senior high and adult students.

Back in Australia I'd noticed a further decline in civility not just in schools but society in general. Political discourse didn't seem possible any more without personal insult, whether in parliament, on radio or anonymously on online forums.

We returned to Japan in 2012. For me it was with a huge sense of relief. In quieter moments of my teaching life or taking the train or riding my bike, I'd give the concept of civility a great deal of thought. I mused about ego and the West's emphasis on the rights of the individual, even to the detriment of everyone else.

Take the concept of humility. It's not exactly *à la mode* in western culture right now and the obsession with individual rights and a universe which seems to revolve about the point 'me.' A prime example is gift giving. A Japanese person handing over a *purezento* or *giftu* (both English words have managed to weasel their way into their language) will say something like *"Kore wa tsumaranai mono desuga, yorosikattara douzo."* A general translation of this might be "Here's a little something. I hope you like it." But a literal translation would yield "This is something worthless. Nevertheless I would be grateful if you accepted it." My Japanese friend tells me confidentially that this is in stark contrast to what Americans do. "They are very generous, neh?" he says, "but they say 'I hope you like this present. It was very expensive and difficult to find. Please look after it.'"

The Japanese have a word *sumimasen*. It's the Swiss army knife of word tools. It can mean variously 'excuse me', 'thank you' or 'sorry', depending on context. You won't go anywhere in Japan without hearing it hundreds of times a day – in the streets, shops, buses, trains, schools and workplace.

When you think about it, English expressions of regret and apology are also steeped in medieval traditions of fealty, obligation and hierarchy. "Excuse me" (please *forgive* me) and "I *beg* your pardon" (no one begs for anything any more and only Texas governors grant pardons – and that happens rarely).

This emphasis on politeness isn't just habit. It's built into the language, a language where even the basic necessities of life are given a kind of reverence with the prefix "O" which is usually translated in English as "honorable" or "polite form". This simple prefix for the basics "O- mizu (water), O-cha (tea) and O-kome (uncooked rice) means that you're constantly showing politeness and respect – even having an everyday mundane conversation.

Japanese is an ancient, incredibly complex language yet very beautiful and poetic. As a poet I'm always impressed at the visual representation of symbols (for example the word for autumn is a combination of the symbols for "tree" and "fire". If you're ever privileged to see a forest of Japanese maples on a mountain in autumn you'll appreciate how appropriate these kanji symbols are. These ideographs have their origins in ancient Chinese – even if the spoken word no longer bears any resemblance.

Although the Japanese word for New Year is 'O-shogatsu', Japanese people wished us Happy New Year by saying "Akemashite Omedetou Gozaimasu!" Only one Kanji character is found in this expression, inside the first word. This Kanji is a combination of the characters for sun and moon. One of the traditional meanings concerns the sun and the moon uniting and becoming "bright", involving "changing, "opening" and "dawning".

Under the lunar calendar of former times, the New Year was seen in relation to change in both the sun and moon and the symbolic nature of light. So "Akemashite Omedetou Gozaimasu" might be roughly translated as "The year is changing… darkness gives way to light… new life begins… Congratulations!"

The point of this is that politeness, respect and civility aren't just social mores in Japan – they're actually built into the structure of the language.

My *kocho-sensei* or principal returned to work after being hospitalized for pneumonia. I tried to say 'welcome back' using *yokoso* (welcome), so my colleague Ikuko deftly jumped in and acted as translator. Even the most pathetic attempt at Japanese is praised and warmly regarded. My sad attempts at the many-layered intricacies of the Japanese language will never prompt outright laughter (although no doubt there's a chuckle to be had privately later at my clumsy attempts). Through her, my principal asked how I was enjoying Japan in general and his school in particular. I answered honestly that I was loving it and that his students were hard-working and friendly. His body-language indicated that he was anxious to move on, so I finished by saying *ki o tsukete* (be careful / take care of yourself). He seemed impressed and replied, "*Yoroshiku*."

Now this word is even more multi-tasking than *sumimasen*. Its full form is *yoroshiku o neigai shimasu*. When people meet for the first time it's a common expression. It means something like "nice to meet you" or *hajime mashite* (I am meeting you for the first time). But I'd met the principal several times before, so this seemed to be inappropriate for the situation.

This is where it gets a little complicated, since, as far as I've been able to determine, there is no equivalent to *yoroshiku o neigai shimasu* in English! Its literal meaning is "I humbly ask you to be kind to me" but there are many more nuanced levels of meaning underlying this literal translation.

The first part of this expression comes from the adjective *yoroshii* (meaning 'good, approved, desirable or convenient'). *"O"* is a prefix of politeness, hence "humble", *"negai"* (wish or hope), *"shi"* (the verb 'to do'), and *"masu"*, another verb of politeness. So what this relatively short expression conveys is something like "I hope you will take care of someone or something in a manner which is convenient for both you and me. I count on your cooperation!" For me that whole expression seemed to sum up the Japanese system of mutual bonds of obligation and caring which has ensured the perpetuation of this culture for thousands of years.

*　　*　　*

After the principal left I asked my colleague Ikuko what she thought *kocho-sensei* meant exactly by *Yoroshiku*.

She hesitated, thinking – a common preamble to any explanation by Japanese – then tilted her head to the side, bird-like, in that oh-so-Japanese idiosyncratic expression of inquiring and deep consideration. "Maybe," she said (also a common precursor to any explanation, as it would be arrogant to give a definitive answer) "Maybe he's saying "Thankyou in advance."

This is taking courtesy to its natural conclusion, isn't it? – "I thank you now for whatever kindness you may extend to me in the future."

It was a brief encounter which led to a lot of reflection on the subtleties of the Japanese language. Once again I was left thinking "*zen zen wakarimasen* – I really don't understand anything. But I'm glad to be here."

Correction

Captain of the ship. A grandiose title, that. Both 'ship' and 'captain' coming from the ancient nautical terms way back to their earthbound roots.

Li Win was more interested in the etymology than the job. She smiled ironically at *Captain* – she had no delusions that she was anything other than a technician in sole charge of this ship which had never sailed through water or air.

Her 99 year contract was to chart a 3.7 parsec sector of Andromeda.

She mused. The legally correct sentence would be "*Its* 99 year contract was to chart a 3.7 parsec sector of Andromeda." Sexist personal pronouns were outlawed now but *she* still referred to *her*self in the retrospeak which had made a comeback in *her* late teens at the turn of the new millennium.

Hmm… 'Chart' – another old marine term…

Essentially she was to take readings of significant matter – planets, moons, dust clouds – so the egg-heads could compare them to the spectral analysis readouts back at the lab just beyond Saturn. Something to do with testing the curve of light in gravitational fields.

So here she was. One ship, no crew. There were tens of thousands of these craft all doing the same work. Some of the Reps on Jupiter said this Pure Research was a waste of taxpayers' money. Others argued that practical inventions and discoveries were often stumbled upon during these theoretical missions, so it was worth every Yuan. For all Li knew, she might just as well be doing geological surveys for later mineral exploration. Whatever. Li wasn't complaining. She was being paid an exorbitant amount just to push buttons. She was at the beginning of her career. She was only 29 years old.

The earth is deserted yet we still use the word 'year' every day. Day. There's another one...

OMG i love the way even words have a past. Even God! No one believes in the entity anymore but it's still in the patois. Supposedly created the heavens and the earth in six days.

Li Win's allotted lifespan was 400 years. After this contract — only ninety years to go — she'd live off her earnings for decades. Maybe slum it on one of the Warm Planets.

Her 'work' was completed in less than a Terran hour every day. Most of the new captains were cyborg. Li was one of the few Entire Hominids to still have the job. When she'd started it was Humans Only, with a strict gender-equity policy at every intake. Since those days of course, gender had become almost irrelevant. After the mapping of the genome at the dawn of the Third Millennium, change had been exponential. Mutation was increased in frequency and range by ionic irradiation of the proteins in RNA. Gene-architects selected the best strands and formulated designs to a blueprint approved by the Ethics Institute. Hereditary mental and physical diseases were mere memories of the bestial past. Once it was discovered that reproduction could be done much more efficiently *ex utero*, women finally achieved the liberation for which they'd yearned for generations. *Generation. Another antiquated word.*

After sex and reproduction became totally independent of each other, sex could be used for recreation.

This was fine, except that a number of sex-related epidemics and pandemics reduced Terra's population by 2/3 in less than a century. As the history files had told Li Win at High School, this was a bigger and better pandemic than the Black Death of the Second Millennium and Avian HIV, the supervirus which evolved in the early years of the Third Millennium. *"Shocking as this new disease was"*, Li remembered the file by rote, *"it simultaneously solved both the problem of too many people and too few resources and coincided with the depletion of fossilised energy. It also challenged our scientists to come up with new methods of sex. Early work on pleasure centres in the brain and the transmission of physical and emotional sensations, first by infrared, then by n waves, excited the populace. At first available only to the wealthiest Chinese, within fifty years the technology was being made in the Third World sweatshops of USA and Sweden. Soon everyone could afford Brain Sex. Mild arousal to orgasm was to be achieved by chemical and electrical stimulation of the septum pellucidium and the hypothalamus ("pleasure centres"). An Amendment to the Sex Act of 2469 has mandated the complete phasing out of genitalia by 3030."*

*   *   *

Li sighs. Just thinking the words Brain Sex remind her of the need. Like when she'd spend hours composing one poem and the time would flow like minutes. Then suddenly she'd realise that she hadn't eaten for six hours and was ravenous. Sex was the same. It must be over forty hours.

The craft is of that old-style with the large bubble port-hole on the bow underside. It gives a wide enough aspect that if she stands close the frame goes beyond her peripheral vision and the craft disappears. It's as if she's moving forward through the vastness of space without the need of a craft at all.

Window she thinks. From the Old Norse. *Wind's eye... Only faint solar winds here...*

She wears only the tight soil-repellent fabric two-piece jumpsuit. It's comfortable and no underwear is required. Every few days residues of perspiration and body oils are eliminated in the eSolvent Cleansing Unit. The only time she wears it though is for the twice-weekly vidlink back to Jupiter.

The vidlink is a brief one. There's nothing to report. She exchanges small talk with the Communications Operative. The need to converse regularly for mental hygiene and morale is recognised by The State, but Li knows that the pseudo-hominid CO is generating speech in response to her initiatives and she never finds it satisfying.

As soon as the link is broken she removes the two halves of the suit. First the top half, crossing her slim arms, grabbing the front of the bottom hem, lifting and uncrossing over her smooth skinned head. She always does this quickly so that her small breasts bounce just once and throws the top toward the instrument panel. Then, by contrast, she slowly removes the tight pants, easing them down over her pressed-together knees and calves until the garment sits on the deck, a sloughed skin around one ankle. Then she kicks it lightly to join its upper-half mate, both floating and pulsing amoeba-like around the cabin.

This slow striptease is for her eyes only. She looks at her image in the selfmonitor, part critically, part admiringly.

She runs her hands over her small hairless body, almost-prepubescent breasts, over her clearly-defined abs and tiny waist. She stands modestly, coquettishly, one knee turned towards the other. Then she stands legs wide apart, hands on narrow hips, chin thrust forward aggressively. She laughs at herself.

She loves this feeling of freedom. Showing off her lean body to the entire universe yet to no living being.

She cups one hand over her almost-smooth pubis where once, in a bestial past, there would have been genitals. Genitalia were vestigial and would eventually evolve themselves out of existence. Meanwhile most fems chose cosmetic surgery to enhance general smoothness and attractiveness. Unfortunately humans still maintained a reliance on kidney filtration for optimal functioning. For the time being the tiny urethra opening was unavoidable.

Li Win is not disappointed that she postponed the clitori-dectomy. The approved method of arousal is via cranial electrodes. She smiles as she remembers her discovery of a better method in the early days of her journey…

She takes a deep breath and lets it out slowly as she faces the interactive screen, makes a C with her thumb and four fingers to indicate 'Correction' to the Main Processing Unit, then taps her index finger mid-air to register Enter on the gesture-reader.

The Coordinate Correction programme activates.

Li Win sits on the control panel as the miniature fusion reactor engages the thrusters and the whole control console vibrates with a tingling hum.

Just a few minutes every day is enough to correct the craft's course and simultaneously send waves of pleasure flooding up through her bottom and groin, the thrumming reaching every nook and cranny of her athletic body.

This is the part that Li Win loves the most. The palms of her hands sliding, pushing her small breasts upwards, twiddling the nipples, fine-tuning her body.

Naked and powerful with the whole constellation of Andromeda before her.

Outwardly motionless, inwardly an exploding supernova.

Thrusting silently and eternally forward into the Void.

Acknowledgements

Tolerance was first published as *Celibacy, Tolerance, Time* in Transnational Literature (May, 2013.) It is based on the story of Hara Tanzan (1819 – 1892) who was both head monk of Saijoji temple and Professor of Philosophy at University of Tokyo. Apparently a man of great wisdom and gentle humour, Tanzan was instrumental in the modernization of Japanese Buddhism and an advocate of merging western science and medicine into Zen Buddhism. There are a number of famous and well-loved tales of Tanzan (mostly apocryphal!). My story is a totally fabricated extension of a single paragraph anecdotal koan sometimes referred to as 'The Muddy Road', re-imagined in the first-person voice. The embellishments are based on some of my own wanderings in Japan.

Bo peep first appeared on the Verity La website in April 2015

lines written on the train between Himeji and Shirahama appeared in Transnational Literature (Flinders Uni, SA) Vol 8 No 2 (May 2016)

retired banker in a nursing home was in fourW twenty four NEW WRITING 2013 (ed. David Gilbey), Wagga Wagga NSW, and editor's choice in Poetry Magazine.com (Vol XIV No. 2, Summer 2013)

Mirror was first published as *Mirrored Image* in Bewildering Stories (Issue #566, April, 2014)

The River appeared in fourW #27 New Writing 2016 (ed. David Gilbey) fourW Press, Wagga Wagga, NSW

crying at the poetry reading premiered in Red River Review (Nov 2011) and was included in the tropeland collection.

The Question was shortlisted for the 2016 Trudy Graham / Julie Lewis Literary Award for Prose and was published in Happy[2] (ed. Matt Potter), Pure Slush Books, Jan 2018

onsen song was published as an audio poem with my original music in Australian Poetry Journal 4.2 http://apj.australianpoetry.org/issues/apj-unthemed-4-2/digital-works/ and on Soundcloud https://soundcloud.com/auspoetry/song-of-an-onsen

Running out of time was first published in the anthology Short and Twisted 2011 (Celapene Press), broadcast on Writers' Radio (Radio Adelaide 101.5 FM) and later adapted as a radio drama podcast on The Drama Pod: http://thedramapod.com/drupal/

The torture of Yahia was published by Al Mannarah Independent Iraqi Newspaper 17/06/06 in English and Arabic and in Australia by Famous Reporter #33 (Walleah Press, Aug 2006)

The bird leaves its cage and enters another appeared in Blue Giraffe 3 (ed. Peter Macrow), June, 2006, in the micromacro collection

A Clarity of Smog first appeared in foam:e #11, and also found its way into tropeland

Your Life © was first read publicly at Spring Shorts / Quart Short Literary Night (Bibliotheca, Adelaide, Oct 17, 2017)

mr miles and *up here on Swanston* were both in the inaugural print edition of malevolent soap (ed. Felix Garner Davis), Oct, 2017

Lost in trainstation was shortlisted for the 2016 Lane Cove Literary Awards and subsequently published in Lane Cove Literary Awards – An Anthology (Lane Cove Library, 2016)

Roly Poly Pudding was initially published in Staples #8 (ed. Shannon Burns), March 2007

Cigarette was first published in Transnational Literature (Volume 7 Issue 1, November 2014)

A house of cards: An earlier version *'The autistic boy'* was published in Mindfields (ed. Ken Vincent & Jude Aquilina), Ginninderra Press. The revised version was collected in Original Clichés.

crabbing from james well to rogues point first appeared in Rabbit Poetry Journal (ed. Jessica Wilkinson) #19 Dec 2016

Through a glass, darkly was published in Greed (ed. Matt Potter), Pure Slush Books, August 2018

cold caller appeared in Zodiac Review (Nov, 2015)

kenny's gun debuted in the zine Story, a living, breathing part of our life – Reflections on space and place by visitors to Once and Again Café (ed. Michele Fairbairn) and published with the assistance of The City of Marion (Mar, 2018)

The first day (memoir) in Do nuns wear knickers? – True stories of school life and what we really learned. (ed. Kari O'Gorman), Melaleuca Blue Publishing, 2016.
It was also broadcast on ABC Radio National's Life Matters, Feb 6, 2017.

Toppin' y'self (earlier version) was published in Freak (ed. Matt Potter), Pure Slush Books, Dec 2016

Holding on debuted at Tenx9 (Adelaide) 'Crush', The Jade, 16/8/18.

The essay *Civility* was broadcast on Ockham's Razor, ABC Radio National 10/05/15. Transcript published on ABC and Radio Australia websites

Correction was first published in Between the sheets (18 short stories from the Stringybark Erotic Fiction Awards, ed. David Vernon) Stringybark Publishing, Smashwords digital edition, Mar 2012. http://www.smashwords.com/books/view/137402 Hard-copy edition, April 2012

My sincere gratitude to all of the editors and producers. All other works are published for the first time.

Thanks

to Mike Ladd, Rachael Mead, Peter Goldsworthy, Carol Le Fevre, Ali Flett, Matt Potter, Don Webb, Maggie Ball, Tim Heffernan, Amelia Walker, Yahia al Samaway, Juan Garrido-Salgado, Ralph Wessman, Robin Williams and the ABC, Michelle Seminara, Stephen Dando-Collins, all my friends in our Poetica poetry workshop, the late Frank Vanehouse, Mrs Vick, The Once and Again authors group and – as always – my family.

Rob Walker, August, 2018

About the Author

Rob Walker didn't begin writing seriously until the mid 1990s. Since then he has published hundreds of poems online and in print in Australia, New Zealand, USA, India, Ireland, Scotland, England and the Middle East, on air and on CD. His poems have been interpreted by the Zephyr String Quartet, performed with MaxMo (an Adelaide-based collective of poets and jazz musos) and translated into Spanish, Arabic, Dutch, Japanese and Chinese. He has had spoken-word, poems and music broadcast on ABC Radio and CD.

Rob also writes occasional poetry reviews and essays, and makes his work available on ccmixter.org, where it has been remixed by musicians in many countries. He has recently begun to focus on short fiction and memoir.

In recent years Rob and his partner taught English to senior-high and university students in Himeji, Japan and now live permanently in Adelaide, South Australia.

Find Rob's website at www.robwalkerpoet.com.

Also by Rob Walker

Original Clichés, Ginninderra Press, Port Adelaide, SA
http://www.ginninderrapress.com.au/ 2016
ISBN-10: 1760411272 ISBN-13: 978-1760411275

tropeland, Five Islands Press, University of Melbourne
Parkville Vic. www.fiveislandspress.com 2015
ISBN: 978-0-7340-5026-7

micromacro, Seaview Press, 2006
ISBN 978-174-008-415-4

sparrow in an airport, New Poets Ten, Friendly Street
Poets/Wakefield Press, 2005.
ISBN 1 86254 670 3

Thirty, (co-edited with Louise Nicholas)
Friendly Street Poets anthology / Wakefield Press, 2006
ISBN 1 86254 702 5

gods for a new world, Ginninderra Press Pocket Poets, 2018

policies & procedures, Southern-Land Poets, Garron
Publishing, Magill, SA, 2015
ISSN 2202-7246

phobiaphobia, Picaro Press, 2007
ISBN 978-1-920957-35-3

Also from TRUTH SERUM PRESS

https://truthserumpress.net/catalogue/

 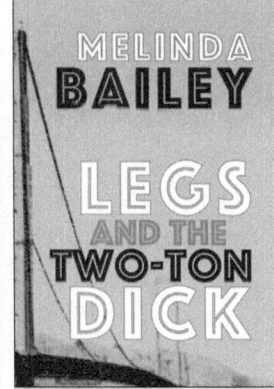 

- *The Crazed Wind* by Nod Ghosh
  978-1-925536-58-4 (paperback) 978-1-925536-59-1 (eBook)
- *Legs and the Two-Ton Dick* by Melinda Bailey
  978-1-925536-37-9 (paperback) 978-1-925536-38-6 (eBook)
- *Cheat Sheets* by Edward O'Dwyer
  978-1-925536-60-7 (paperback) 978-1-925536-61-4 (eBook)

- *On the Bitch* by Matt Potter
  978-1-925536-45-4 (paperback) 978-1-925536-46-1 (eBook)
- *Kiss Kiss* by Paul Beckman
  978-1-925536-21-8 (paperback) 978-1-925536-22-5 (eBook)
- *Dollhouse Masquerade* by Samuel E. Cole
  978-1-925536-21-8 (paperback) 978-1-925536-22-5 (eBook)

Also from TRUTH SERUM PRESS

https://truthserumpress.net/catalogue/

 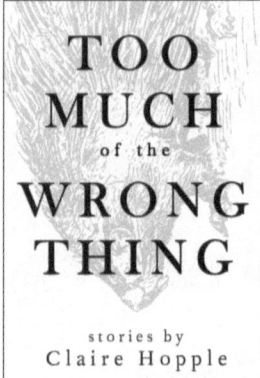 

- *Inklings* by Irene Buckler
  978-1-925536-41-6 (paperback) 978-1-925536-42-3 (eBook)
- *Too Much of the Wrong Thing* by Claire Hopple
  978-1-925536-33-1 (paperback) 978-1-925536-34-8 (eBook)
- *Track Tales* by Mercedes Webb-Pullman
  978-1-925536-35-5 (paperback) 978-1-925536-36-2 (eBook)

 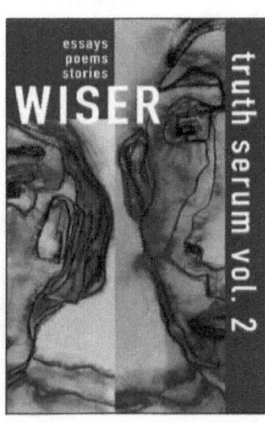 

- *True Truth Serum Vol. #1*
  978-1-925536-29-4 (paperback) 978-1-925536-30-0 (eBook)
- *Wiser Truth Serum Vol. #2*
  978-1-925536-31-7 (paperback) 978-1-925536-32-4 (eBook)
- *What Came Before* by Gay Degani
  978-1-925536-05-8 (paperback) 978-1-925536-06-5 (eBook)

Also from TRUTH SERUM PRESS

https://truthserumpress.net/catalogue/

- *Hello Berlin!* by Jason S. Andrews
  978-1-925536-11-9 (paperback) 978-1-925536-12-6 (eBook)
- *Deer Michigan* by Jack C. Buck
  978-1-925536-25-6 (paperback) 978-1-925536-26-3 (eBook)
- *Rain Check* by Levi Andrew Noe
  978-1-925536-09-6 (paperback) 978-1-925536-10-2 (eBook)

- *Luck and Other Truths* by Richard Mark Glover
  978-1-925101-77-5 (paperback) 978-1-925536-04-1 (eBook)
- *The Miracle of Small Things* by Guilie Castillo Oriard
  978-1-925101-73-7 (paperback) 978-1-925101-74-4 (eBook)
- *La Ronde* by Townsend Walker
  978-1-925101-64-5 (paperback) 978-1-925101-65-2 (eBook)

www.ingramcontent.com/pod-product-compliance
Lightning Source LLC
Chambersburg PA
CBHW050825180626
46814CB00004B/1464